I0542459

OPERATOR 5:
INVASION OF THE YELLOW WARLORDS

INVASION OF THE YELLOW WARLORDS

By Curtis Steele

STEEGER BOOKS • 2020

© 1935, 2020 Argosy Communications, Inc. All rights reserved.
Authorized and produced under license.

PUBLISHING HISTORY

"Invasion of the Yellow Warlords" originally appeared in the June, 1935 (Vol. 4, No. 3) issue of *Operator #5* magazine. Copyright © 2020 by Argosy Communications, Inc. All rights reserved.

ALL RIGHTS RESERVED

No part of this book may be reproduced or utilized in any form or by any means, electronic or mechanical, without permission in writing from the publisher.

This edition has been marked via subtle changes, so anyone who reprints from this collection is committing a violation of copyright.

Visit STEEGERBOOKS.COM for more books like this.

CHAPTER 1
HELL'S HEAT

THE WHITE shaft of a searchlight shot upward from the superstructure of the U.S. Battleship *Oklahoma,* swinging like a brandished sword, and played on the glittering wings of a Navy bomber circling high in the night sky.

Beneath spread the trackless, black expanse of the Pacific, unmarked save by the boiling wakes of the great ships of the U.S. Pacific Fleet as they steamed in line formation toward the North, away from San Diego Bay.

Their funnels poured out smoke as black as the night; their beacons twinkled on the barrels of their huge guns; steadily they ploughed on while the knifelike beam of the searchlight slashed the sky, cutting a way through the darkness for the descending Navy bomber.

Three passengers stood, crowded together, in the observation pit of the swift plane. Helmets hooded them; goggles protected their eyes; all three wore fur-lined coveralls. Peering down through the darkness, they studied the parade of steel sea-monsters cleaving the swells below.

It was a sight they had been awaiting anxiously during the long, nerve-straining hours of their one-stop flight from Bolling Field, Washington, D.C. A fast Army plane had whisked them west from there; at the San Diego Naval Training Station they had transferred to the amphibian plane, and at last it was spiral-

ing them down toward their goal, the pitching flagship of the Pacific Fleet. Special orders from the General Staff of the Army and Navy had cleared all airways for them.

One of the men, who sat particularly alert beside his two companions, turned puzzled eyes into the depths of the engulfing night. His face shone, clean-cut, in the glow of the instrument-board; behind the lenses of his goggles his blue eyes gleamed darkly. He was in his early twenties, yet it was plain

Utter destruction struck the ships of the fleet.

that he possessed a confidence, a poise beyond his years. He was American to the core.

Abruptly he straightened, and his gloved hand shot out to slap the shoulder of the pilot at the controls in the fore pit.

"Stay up!" he commanded through the drone of the engine. "Circle!"

The Navy pilot had likewise begun to look about with troubled eyes; now he immediately obeyed the command and dressed his ship. The bomber leaned on one wing, maintaining altitude while the shaft of the searchlight followed it. The young man in the observation cubby glanced at his companions. From their mystified expressions it seemed they too had sensed that something strange was happening. Suddenly the plane was flying through air as warm as that of the tropics.

The young man drew off his right glove and touched the spider of the microphone connected to the short-wave radio equipment. The article was warm—astonishingly so—and quickly becoming warmer. He zipped open the front of his coveralls and his supple fingers sought a golden ornament attached to his watch-chain. The keen darkness of his eyes deepened when he touched it.

The watch-charm was cunningly fashioned into a death's head, its eyes formed by brilliant rubies. And at this moment it, too, was startlingly hot.

The companion on his right suddenly jerked off his own glove, peered at a ring of white metal on his finger. Its emblem was a picture of the golden death-charm—a skull of white emblazoned against a black background, its forehead marked by the mystic numeral 5. He tugged at it, and blurted into the wind: "It's getting hotter every second!"

IT WAS true. A strange heat was enveloping the entire plane, a mounting, oppressive warmth which even the flow of air did not carry away. It radiated from the wings, from every metal part of the fuselage; penetrated into the bodies of the three passengers and the pilot, bringing with it the oppressive sensation of a fever. Abruptly the coolness of the night had vanished, and the plane had plunged into this strange pocket of heat—heat that mounted swiftly.

The young man who had first noted the strange phenomenon felt, inside his coveralls, his arm-pitted automatic growing hotter. Beside him, his one companion began a quick attempt to remove the mystic ring, evidently becoming a source of sharp pain. Then his other companion suddenly tore off goggles that radiated stinging heat. The pilot ripped open his coveralls, peered about, puzzled, and touched metal that snapped as it expanded.

"Deadhead!" the command rang in his ears. "Full throttle—south!"

Swiftly the plane banked, leveled, roared above the line of plunging ships while the shaft of the searchlight swept after it. For a few seconds the startling heat phenomenon followed it through the sky. Then, as suddenly and as strangely as it had come, it vanished—the oppressiveness left the air; the metal parts of the plane began to cool; the feverishness faded from the bodies of the pilot and the three passengers. Again the night became crisply cold.

The young man in the observation cubby searched anew the depths of the night. His two companions gazed at him strangely, but he did not speak. The pilot stared back a request for instructions. He gave them.

"Head for the *Oklahoma!*"

The bomber whipped about, roared under full power until it reached a position above the flagship of the Pacific Fleet. The swinging searchlight still followed as it planed down and settled gracefully upon the waves.

From the steel side of the *Oklahoma* a power-boat swerved, tracing a white path across the swells to the teetering plane. It swung carefully alongside, and the three passengers quickly transferred to it.

"Return to your base!" the bomber's pilot was ordered.

The power-boat churned back toward its mother ship. As it pitched, the three passengers stripped out of their coveralls. The young man, garbed impeccably in a tailored business suit, watched the lights of the *Oklahoma* gleam close as his fingers strayed again, this time unconsciously, to the golden death-charm he wore—which was now cool.

His one companion, a boy in his teens, pulled an old cap with a broken bill from his hip pocket and slipped it upon his tousled head. He was a tough looking lad, with a face spotted by freckles, a pugnacious tilted nose. Looking back to see the Navy bomber swooping off the swells, he asked breathlessly:

"Gee, Jimmy what was it? What happened up there?"

"Something very strange, Tim. That's all I can say now."

THE OTHER passenger also stepped out of the coveralls and tugged on an impertinent looking hat. She too was in her early twenties; obviously a self-reliant young woman quite capable of taking care of herself in any emergency. Just now though she wore a puzzled expression. Adjusting flying tendrils of hair, straightening her smart suit, she said:

"Sometimes a swimmer finds himself in colder water all of a sudden. One moment the water will be very warm, and the next, surprisingly chilly. Was it something like that, Jimmy—did we pass into a cloud of very warm air?"

6

"Perhaps, Di," the young man answered, "but on the other hand—perhaps it can't be explained so easily."

The power-boat chugged against the steel hulk of the *Oklahoma*. Quickly the three passengers mounted the accommodation ladder. They paused, facing three smartly uniformed officers; the young man and the boy saluted. Rear-Admiral Walton, Commander of the flagship of the Pacific Fleet, stated quietly:

"I have radio advice from Major-General Falk, Chief of Staff, to expect you at this time."

"My credentials, sir."

The smartly dressed young man withdrew a thin silver case from his pocket. The pressure of his thumbnail on a concealed spring in one corner of it released a catch, and a thin leaf sprang up. He proffered it, and Rear-Admiral Walton read the letter framed inside it:

THE WHITE HOUSE
Washington

To Whom It May Concern:
The identity of the bearer of this letter must be kept strictly confidential.

He is Operator 5 of the United States Intelligence Service.

The signature affixed to the credential was that of the President of the United States.

Rear-Admiral Walton returned the case and gripped the hand of Operator 5.

"I consider it an honor to meet you. I have heard many times

of your great service to our country." He turned briskly. "Captain
Hunter and Lieut. Commander
Hall, this is Operator 5 of the
Intelligence—but you must keep
his identity a strict secret from our
brother officers."

James Christopher—whose
name was entered in the secret
archives of the Intelligence Service beside the designation of
Operator 5—gripped the hands of the two men.

"Miss Diane Elliot," he introduced, and the officers bowed
to the girl. "She is a special reporter for the Amalgamated Press
Service, and she obtained permission from the War Department to come aboard the *Oklahoma* tonight. And Tim Donovan, gentlemen—too young to be officially listed as a member
of the Intelligence, but unofficially as valuable as any operator
in the service."

"I have heard of you, too," Admiral Walton declared as he
gripped the tough little Irish lad's hard hand. "If you will come
with me—"

He conducted them to the bridge companionway, mounted
after them. Beyond misted panes of glass spread the black sea;
behind the *Oklahoma,* plowing through the swells in majestic
parade, the other great ships of the Pacific Fleet were spangled
with the colors of their beacons.

Operator 5, turning, found the Commander's face graven
deep with anxiety. "I have been instructed," he said, "to learn at

first hand the details of the destruction of the battleship *California* at dawn today."

THE MERE mention of the destroyed battleship made Admiral Walton pale. His officers, as they stood beside him on the bridge, appeared baffled and worn.

"The news of the destruction of the *California* early this morning has startled the entire nation," Operator 5 added quietly. "General Staff is bewildered by your report. Is it true, Commander Walton, that you cannot state the cause of the sudden sinking of that ship?"

"The fate of that ship," Admiral Walton answered stiffly, "is absolutely unparalleled in naval history. Nothing like it has ever happened before. I cannot explain it, nor can any of my officers. I have already informed General Staff of all the details known to me. The *California* is as baffling a mystery of the sea as *The Black Prince*." *

"The *California* was destroyed in full sight of every other ship

---

* AUTHOR'S NOTE: The *Black Prince,* a British cruiser, participated in the famous battle of Jutland with the *Defense* and the *Warrior.* These three cruisers steamed into the thick of this celebrated naval battle. A moment after they came under fire from the guns of the enemy, flame poured from the fore-turret of the *Black Prince* and an immense column of fire shot up, together with smoke, debris and spray. After the mist cleared off the water, there was no sign of the ship. It had been blown to bits along with the entire crew. At the same time the *Warrior* was hit powerfully and turned out of the battle only to sink the following morning. The *Black Prince* is one of the great mysteries of the sea. With 250 ships crowding about, she disappeared

of the fleet, was it not?" Operator 5 persisted, sensing a sudden hostility on the part of Admiral Walton. "Her commander had an opportunity to radio you a warning before she plunged to the bottom."

"His message," Admiral Walton snapped, "explains nothing."

He slipped a copy of a wireless communication from a pocket and proffered it. Operator 5's eyes sharpened at the few terse lines:

STRANGE HEAT ENVELOPING SHIP—ALL METAL TOO HOT TO TOUCH—GUNNERY OFFI- CERS REPORT MAGAZINES SIZZLING—EXPLO- SION IMMINENT UNLESS

The message ended abruptly. Operator 5 raised glittering eyes to those of Admiral Walton. The Commander said coldly:

"The report was never completed. At the instant the word 'unless' came through, the *California* was torn apart by a terrific explosion. When the fumes cleared away there was absolutely no sign of her. She went to the bottom leaving neither a trace of herself nor of her crew."

"It is quite impossible, is it not," Operator 5 inquired evenly, "that the sudden heat which destroyed the *California* was due to a fire aboard her?"

"Quite impossible!" Commander Walton snapped. "Every one of her magazines exploded at the same instant. She was

completely, with seven officers and more than eight hundred sailors aboard. No bodies nor wreckage were ever found to explain her fate.

literally ripped to bits, from stem to stern, in a second. No fire could possibly have caused the amazing condition of the *California* an instant before she blew up."

"And that condition, Commander, was—?"

"Every square inch of that ship, above the water line, was shining red hot!"

OPERATOR 5 stepped forward alertly. "You're positive of that? You saw—?"

"It was a sight none of us will ever forget!" the Commander blurted. "It was still very dark. The *California* was holding the rear position in the line formation. When Commander Nelson's message began to come in, I turned my binoculars upon it. I saw at once that the radio antenna was shining in the dark, as though white hot."

"Yes?"

"The glow began to spread over the entire ship while I watched—in a few seconds. Captain Hunter and Lieutenant Hall saw exactly the same thing. Then the turrets began to glow red hot. The rails stood out like lines of fire. The guns began to gleam. I saw men running in terror across the decks, and I swear before God their shoes were flaming—because the deck was sizzling. Steam began to envelop the whole ship—steam from the water around her. The sea was boiling!"

"This," Jimmy Christopher asked quietly, "happened very swiftly?"

"Swiftly?" Admiral Walton repeated in a husky tone. "Before God, that ship began to shine in the dark like an iron just taken from a bed of coals, all in a few seconds!"

11

"None of the other ships of the fleet," Jimmy Christopher inquired, "have encountered this strange force?"

"Thank God they have not!"

"But there is no reason to believe that another of them might not meet it—at any moment?"

The Admiral's face grew whiter. Dark lines deepened in the anxious faces of the officers standing beside him. Operator 5 turned, peered again at the glimmering beacons of the ships of the line.

"If that strange power, whatever it is," he said quietly, should strike again, if more of our ships should be destroyed in that same strange way—it would, at the least, gravely disrupt the Pacific naval war games, would it not?" *

Admiral Walton could not answer. Operator 5 turned to him

---

* AUTHOR'S NOTE: The most gigantic war games ever staged in naval history, according to dispatches circulated throughout the United States last December, were scheduled to be launched on May 3 by the United States fleet in the Pacific, under plans developed by Admiral Joseph M. Reeves, Commander-in-chief.

"The fleet," these dispatches said, "will use two-thirds of the northern Pacific Ocean as their field, ranging from the westernmost tip of the Aleutian Islands to the tropics, and from the Pacific Coast of continental United States to Midway Island, which is nearly 1,200 miles west of Honolulu.

"In the war games there will be the greatest fighting force ever assembled in peace-time under a single command. Included are 177 surface ships, 577 airplanes in the high seas air force, the dirigible Macon and approximately 55,000 officers and men."

briskly, lids lowering, hand straying again unconsciously to the little golden death-charm on his watch-chain.

"Still worse, a repetition of that disaster would seriously cripple the fleet. We are, as it is, operating our Navy under a handicap in a dangerous area where extensive preparations for war by other nations have been going on for many months." *

Admiral Walton blurted: "You can't believe that it will happen again! The destruction of the *California* occurred in such a way that I would not believe it if I had not seen it with my own eyes. To think that the same thing might happen to others of our ships—it's impossible!"

"Impossible?" Operator 5 smiled slowly. "A few moments ago,

---

* AUTHOR'S NOTE: On the day when President Roosevelt placed a wreath upon the tomb of the Unknown Soldier at Arlington, and the Prince of Wales broadcast a poem of peace to the world, the Emperor of the Yellow Empire led at dawn 25,000 troops in the second day of a three-day war game in which the Empire was defended against an "enemy" in the East.

Long accounts of the military actions were published in the *Yellowese* press, vividly illustrated with photographs of night marching, camouflaged machine gun nests, tanks, hospital corps, pontoon bridges, and soup kitchens. The war games came coincident with the rise of a stronger militaristic spirit within the Empire.

Especially disquieting to the large foreign population in the Yellow Empire was the appearance of provocative anti-foreign posters plastered on telephone poles, calling upon the populace to resist commercial encroachments by Western countries and to demand full equality of status for the Yellow Empire in the family of nations.

Admiral Walton, while we were in the Navy bomber, we felt the same strange burst of heat envelope us. We succeeded in escaping it—fortunately, for in a few minutes more that plane would have exploded in midair. You must realize here and now that the *California* was destroyed by some strange power that was turned upon it—"

"A power—that would make a great steel battleship a red hot furnace in a few seconds?" Commander Walton demanded. "What could possibly produce—?"

"Exactly such a power," Jimmy Christopher declared, "and you have seen it at work. I have no authority here, sir, but I must urge you to take every possible precaution. First, order all the Commanders of the line to report to you instantly if they should feel that hellish heat close down on them."

"I cannot believe—"

"You *must* know," Operator 5 declared ringingly, "that if the same power turns upon this entire fleet it will destroy all our sea-power in the Pacific!"

COMMANDER WALTON, swallowing hard, stiffened as if in resentment at the imperative tone. But he only said huskily, "Of course I'll issue those orders," and turned away.

He stopped short as an officer breathlessly appeared from the companionway and gasped: "The watch reports a fleet of battle-ships on the horizon, sir—nationality unknown!"

"What!" Admiral Walton snapped around. "Unknown battleships in the middle of the Pacific? What the devil are you talking about?"

"I've verified it, sir! It's quite true! They are directly west and steaming toward us. I believe, sir, that it is a Yellowese Squadron!"

Commander Walton stood stunned. During the moment of tense quiet that followed, Operator 5 spoke softly:

"Your orders to the ships of the line, Commander! They are more necessary at this moment than—"

Jimmy Christopher broke off as a second officer spun from the companionway and rushed to the Admiral. His face was a ghastly white; his breath beat quickly as he pointed a trembling finger past the misty windows.

"The *Colorado*, sir! Radio message—just received! The Commander reports that the whole ship is becoming heated! Look at it, sir! Look at it!"

Operator 5's alert nerves snapped him first toward the open bridge. As he darted to spray-laden air, peering along the line of twinkling beacons. Commander Walton crowded at this side. Tim Donovan, gripping the rail with whitening fingers, stared with them through the night at the last ships in the mighty battle parade.

Across the rolling swells, the *Colorado* was outlined by a weird glow. The wires of its radio aerial were already white streaks in the dark. Its rails were shining with an uncanny phosphorescence which gradually became brighter. Smoke poured up, blending into the black plumes of the funnels—the fumes of scorching, blistering paint. From stem to stern the great warrior of the deep began to gleam like a sparkling hot iron!

Transfixed with horror, the Commander and his officers stared at the incredible scene. Now the huge guns of the *Colorado* were appearing brighter in the glow—great cannon shining red! The vapor shrouded turrets were becoming radiant hot shells. The funnels shone white. Then the antenna wires parted, dropping like writhing snakes of fire toward the deck on which terrorized men were swarming, with shoes and their uniforms ablaze! Flames swooped in the wind, as all around them the great battleship became a weltering furnace!

Rear-Admiral Walton jerked from the rail, tearing his eyes from the sight. Orders crowded to his lips, but he jerked to a stop, struck with the despairing realization that no mere orders could remove the imminent danger of destruction from the *Colorado.*

Operator 5, hands gripping the rail, looked away from the gleaming craft to peer into the distance—into the west where a squadron of Yellowese fighting boats had been reported sighted.

The *Colorado* was a beacon of hell, floating in the sea. Maddened men were leaping over the rails far too hot to touch, plunging headlong into the steaming ocean. Clouds of steam shrouded the doomed vessel. On the wind and across the swells carried the shrieks of men trapped aboard her, dying a death of horror. For a few long seconds the shining ship plunged on. Then utter destruction struck her.

An explosion that must have sent its force to the core of the earth blasted the *Colorado* to bits. Instantly the ship vanished in flame which sheeted high into the sky, billowed far across the water. Clouds of fumes spread over the waves, streaked with flying fragments of metal that still sparkled white hot. When the wind tore the smoke away from that black whirlpool, no sign of the *Colorado* remained.

Dazedly Admiral Walton peered at the lashing sea where a moment ago the *Colorado* had been proudly riding; speechlessly his officers stared beside him.

Operator 5 turned quickly, eyes darkened to blackness. His voice was edged as he said: "It may strike again! It may turn upon this entire fleet! Commander, I urge you to order your ships out of this area, back toward shore, under full steam!"

Admiral Walton straightened, the muscles of his jaws bunching hard, his hands closed into fists.

"Withdraw? No, sir! The Yellow Squadron is responsible for this! They have destroyed two of my ships! We're going to fight! *Orders!*"

His clipped instructions sent officers running to the telephone and toward the radio room. His call brought other men, whipped them into frenzied action. Through the ether the whine of a wireless oscillator sounded, carrying orders to the other ships of the line. On that surging black sea, great battleships began to swing off their peaceful lane. Out of the west destruction had struck without warning, and toward the west they plunged.

It was a counter-attack!

CHAPTER 2
YELLOW CHALLENGE

O PERATOR 5 stepped tensely toward Admiral Walton, who turned from issuing crackling orders which sent startled officers scrambling off the bridge, and confronted him defiantly. "The destruction of those two ships is an act of war, sir, which can be answered in only one way—battle!"

Jimmy Christopher spoke quietly, yet his words rang as though they were tempered steel. "Commander, I repeat that I realize I have no authority whatever here. I have affronted you by suggesting orders, but the safety of this fleet demands it. Your sending these ships against the Yellow Squadron may mean the utter destruction of every one of them!"

"Sir, I am in command here. I know the force that destroyed the *California* and the *Colorado* came from the Yellowese ships. I know that this whole fleet may be blown up in exactly the same way—*unless we rout or sink the enemy squadron now!*"

"You cannot succeed if—"

"The Yellowese have opened war on us—without a declaration. They are steaming toward our coast at this very minute. It is a planned invasion, sir! It is my duty to stop them!"

"It is not your duty, Commander," Operator 5 declared gently, "to lead your fleet to the bottom of the sea so that the way will be left wide open for the invaders!"

Wrathfully Commander Walton turned from Jimmy Christopher; again he snarled orders at dismayed officers who crowded the companionway.

At that moment a roar throbbed over the sound of his voice—the thunder of battle birds being launched into the vastness of the dark which sheltered the ominous Yellow Squadron.

"The *Lexington* is next in line in formation, sir!" Lieut. Commander Hall gasped. "The loss of the *California* and the *Colorado* has placed it in that position!"

"They will not strike at us a third time now!"

The air shook with the drumming of the fighting planes, springing into the air from the flight-deck of the *Lexington*. The great airplane-carrier, riding the black sea heavily, her foamy wake a white tail to the formation, sent plane after plane into the sky.

Westward they drove, seeking the location of the enemy fleet. Sparkling beacons drew the eyes of the observers in the air. Their voices lightninged back through the night by wireless. With the Yellow Fleet lying below they clicked out cryptic messages, spotting their targets. One by one they plunged upon their mark—and into a hell of anti-aircraft fire.

From the decks of the Yellow Squadron, fast firing guns spat shrapnel. Concussions shook the sky, flinging death-dealing projectiles for hundreds of yards in all directions. As swiftly as the wings of the U.S. birds spread above the Yellowese ships, that swiftly the Oriental gunners answered the challenge with withering bursts that made the sky a howling tornado of death. THE GRAY battle-wagons of the American line plunged, as snapping orders called a broadside attack. In the turrets, gun crews worked frantically. Interlocking doors opened and closed, silk encased destruction swung on cradles to the breeches of the big guns.

Hydraulic rammers pushed heavy charges of the high-explosive home behind fourteen inch projectiles weighing 1,400 pounds. Gunnery officers flashed "Ready!" while turret officers watched their gleaming signal lights. Suddenly voices of doom spoke in an earth-rocking chorus and the great guns leaped in violent recoil.

Screaming shells traced their trajectories across the sky, plunged, and tore the sea with their power. The great ships of the Yellow squadron rocked, and their shrieking projectiles answered the challenge. The light of gun flames flashed across the sea as the battle swiftly mounted to an intensity that, it seemed, would jar the very ocean bed.

Searchlights swung their beams high, seeking birds of war. Anti-aircraft batteries continued to cough hollow reports into the thunderous reports of the big guns.

On the bridge of the *Oklahoma,* Operator 5 peered out into the flashing night through powerful binoculars. The blazing of the Yellowese guns was visible on the horizon. At each broadside, great swells rose. To these Jimmy Christopher gave no glance. He turned his lenses upon the *Lexington*, now bringing up the gray line, and saw planes still launching off the flight deck. He turned, when, through the turmoil of the conflict, he heard the rasping word "submarine" break from the lips of Rear-Admiral Walton.

"Torpedoes are the reason for the sinking of our two ships!" the Commander was snarling as Operator 5 turned to him. "Torpedoes carrying charges of thermite! That damnable stuff has done the damage!"

Jimmy Christopher declared crisply: "Laying down protection against torpedoes will not save you, Commander. Neither ship was struck by a torpedo before it sank. A charge of thermite driven into them would have fused a hole through the hull, but would not have heated them white hot. It's something far different and far more deadly than has—"

"Sir, it is my conclusion that the Yellowese have turned a new type of submarine upon us—a type developed far beyond our own!" *

Jimmy Christopher turned with sudden determination from

---

* AUTHOR'S NOTE: On the subject of submarine naval equipment, a noted authority has stated: "We have the largest submarine fleet of any the leading naval powers—and the worst! Most of our submarines were contracted for in our early World War program and consequently we lost the chance to incorporate in them the results of war experience. The most effective submarine fleet of today is that of Japan."

the Commander. He slipped a small square of paper from his pocket, wrote on it rapidly, and thrust it at Tim Donovan.

"Take this to the radio room now, Tim! See that it's sent at once!"

As the tough little Irish lad scampered from the bridge, he turned again to peer at the *Lexington*. The flashing light of the roaring guns flickered blindingly upon him; spray rained past his lenses.

Diane Elliot came quickly to his side. Her hand curled tightly around his arm as he cried: "Di, Commander Walton is leading his fleet into a trap. I may be wrong—he is a trained naval expert, and should know. Yet—" He broke off, his voice fading. "I shouldn't have let you come, Di. This ship, any other ship of the line, may go to the bottom at any moment."

THE SHRILL scream of a falling shell cut into his words. The weighty projectile plunged into the water just aft of the *Oklahoma*. A terrific concussion whipped flame and spray high into the air, created a swell that slapped violently against the flagship.

Huddled against the burst of flying water, blinded by it, Operator 5 and Diane Elliot clung to the rail. The girl peered up with widened eyes as the surge of destructive power passed.

"You warned me it might be dangerous before we started, Jimmy," she answered breathlessly. "I came with my eyes open. I'm not afraid."

"Good girl!" Again Operator 5 peered through his binoculars. "The United States has been promised this attack for months. We've watched the Yellow Empire prepare for it—

we've done nothing to ward it off but schedule war-games in the Pacific—and now it has come! Those poor devils up there in these planes—they're being ripped to pieces by shrapnel made from scrap iron bought by the Yellow Empire from the United States!" *

Flame flashed in the sky even as Operator 5 spoke—an American plane enveloped in fire. It screamed downward as the blaze washed back over its wings, plunged like a torch toward the surface. Grimly Jimmy Christopher watched it strike the sea and vanish—a plane destroyed, a pilot killed.

He turned abruptly as Tim Donovan ran to him and tugged at his arm.

"The radio operator refuses to send this message, Jimmy! He won't do it without orders from Commander Walton!"

Operator 5's lips tightened. "Commander Walton will never order this message sent. It means we've got to—"

He broke off suddenly and snapped the binoculars to his eyes, trained them on the giant airplane-carrier plunging at the end of the line. Then he stood rigid. The wireless aerial of the ship was

---

* AUTHOR'S NOTE: Statistical records show that during 1934 the Yellow Empire purchased more scrap iron and steel from the United States than all other nations of the world combined. The metal was, according to reports, being used largely for the manufacture of shrapnel. At the same time, as has already been noted here in previous reports, the Yellow Empire was reported to be buying decommissioned ships from the United States, and converting them into steel for war uses.

beginning to glow. Men on her decks were running frantically. Again the invisible destructive power was striking.

He spun. "Commander Walton!" His ringing voice turned the haggard eyes of the Admiral. "Look at the *Lexington!* Look at it and see that your tactics are not protecting your ships in the slightest!"

The dismayed Commander jerked to the side of Operator 5. Before his eyes the same glow was shining that had presaged the doom of the *California* and the *Colorado*—a glow spreading to envelope completely the airplane-carrier. With each second it brightened, a deadly shine in the night, a warning that again destruction was about to strike.

Fumes began to pour from the outside of her funnels, from the superstructure, from the hull; her paint boiled and blistered. On the flight deck, pilots and officers mobbed madly toward planes that were likewise fuming under the hot power engulfing them. The fat tires of the crates bubbled and melted against a deck rapidly becoming unbearable as a support for the men upon it. Like an image developing on a photographic plate, the *Lexington* became outlined against the darkness, a shining hot thing in a boiling sea!

Fascinated, horror struck, the men on the bridge of the *Oklahoma* watched—dreading the moment when, inevitably, the stroke of doom must sound. They saw riddled planes, returning from the sky battle, sink toward the deck, then soar again as desperate pilots pulled up from certain destruction. They saw other planes attempt to launch off—and plunge, white with the terrific heat, into the steaming sea. They saw crates explode on the deck, planes torn by rending concussions as the fuel in their tanks blazed up. Swiftly, one after another, half a score of crates disintegrated into flaming fragments and then—

Then the bolt of doom struck. An explosion so violent that the thunder of the sea battle vanished beneath it, so terrific that the great *Lexington* became lost in the turmoil of its intensity, shook the surface of the sea. A cosmic burst of flame rolled skyward, and out across the swells. Smoke, blacker than night, spread thickly over the nearer ships in the line. The ocean dropped away beneath the power of the burst forming a maelstrom which lived for a moment then vanished in the white fury of the lashing waves. When the whirlpool vanished, the *Lexington* vanished with it.

THE DESTRUCTION of the giant airplane-carrier brought a moment's lull into the sea battle. The big guns grew silent, as if in awe before a power far greater than theirs. The machine guns stopped sputtering in the crates overhead as the chattering of monkeys stops in fear when the ominous thunder of a lion's roar shakes the jungle.

And on the bridge of the *Oklahoma*, flagship of the fleet which doom had thrice decimated, officers stood mute before the horrible majesty of that power.

Operator 5, turning sharply upon Admiral Walton, was the first to speak. Into that shocked hush he said: "I urge you again, Commander, to order your fleet to withdraw before every one of them, including your flagship, is sent plunging to the bottom of the Pacific!"

Admiral Walton stiffened with desperate determination.

"Our only hope is to rout or destroy the Yellow Squadron! They're still steaming eastward! Driving toward our coast in hopes of opening the way for an invasion! To withdraw now would mean a surrender to them. I cannot countenance that, sir—and I cannot undertake to explain my tactics to a civilian!"

Operator 5's face whitened at the rebuke. He was about to speak when an officer hurried into the bridge, clutching a communication in one hand. Admiral Walton snatched the message from him.

"An air-observer has reported other ships behind the Yellow Squadron!" the officer blurted. "They are mobilized Yellowese merchant marine—loaded with Yellow troops! They're advancing behind the Yellow Squadron and—"

"Invasion!" Admiral Walton repeated vehemently. "They must be stopped! If they break through our line, these troops will flood across our coast and take possession—"

Again Operator 5 spoke ringingly. "Your counter-attack, sir, is opening the way for that invasion! You are inviting the destruction of your entire fleet and that will mean a way opened wide

to the Yellowese expeditionaires! Withdrawal will not stop the invasion but it will preserve battleships which we must not lose!"

Admiral Walton peered glintingly at Jimmy Christopher. "If you voice your opposition to my tactics again, sir," he declared icily, "I will order you thrown into irons. That is final!"

Operator 5's lips pressed tight. Not because he feared now to speak—but because a smoldering fury rendered him wordless.

He turned abruptly to peer out across the flame-ripped darkness, at the dim outlines of the great fighting ship plunging through a stormy sea. His anxious gaze flashed to Diane Elliot, and his hand shot out to the arm of Tim Donovan.

"Stay here, Di! Tim, you're coming with me!"

The breathless Irish lad at his side, he hurried from the bridge. Flickering light played over them—the flame of big guns firing, of machine guns spitting in the sky, of anti-aircraft shells. Operator 5 gripped a knob and, Tim still at his side, stepped alertly into the steel-walled radio room.

Before his instruments the wireless operator perched, his ear-phones clamped tight. He was writing rapidly. Terror shone in his eyes as the point of his pencil flew across his pad.

He swung sharply, to type the message, and quickly, rudely, Operator 5 grabbed it, read it even as the other jerked to his feet in protest.

HEAVY CRUISER NORTHAMPTON REPORTS ENVELOPED BY HEAT RAPIDLY GROWING MORE INTENSE COMMANDER ASKS ORDERS TO SHIFT POSITION OUT OF FORMATION IN HOPE—

JIMMY CHRISTOPHER flung the pad to the table. He took up the pencil, ripped off the sheet, wrote rapidly on a fresh page. He thrust the message into the hands of the frenzied wireless operator.

"Send that at once!"

The operator's eyes flashed. "Against orders! Get the skipper's okay and I'll—"

Jimmy Christopher gripped the man's arm. "That message must be sent now!"

The door opened behind him and he turned, to see Commander Walton standing just inside. The Admiral advanced slowly, his gaze accusing.

The wireless operator exclaimed: "He's asking me to send a message, sir! I've refused, without orders from you!"

Commander Walton's jaw squared as he picked up the message. His eyes glittered as he threw it down violently. He was about to speak when the radio operator nicked before him the communication just received from the *Northampton.*

"Your orders, Clayton," Admiral Walton's voice cracked, "are that that message is not to be sent!"

"Yes, sir!"

Walton's eyes gleamed at Jimmy Christopher. "You, sir, are to consider yourself under arrest!"

The darkness in Operator 5's eyes deepened. His hand had strayed, as if unconsciously, to the golden death-charm he wore. Now, with a sudden movement, he darted that hand inside his coat and brought out a gleaming automatic, pointed it at Commander Walton.

"You leave me no other alternative, sir!" he said crisply. "I must get that message to General Staff."

The startled Commander jerked back, his face red with unspeakable wrath. The radio operator stood motionless, appalled at the sight of a civilian threatening the supreme officer of the fleet. Even Tim Donovan stood chilled with amazement at Jimmy Christopher's act.

For a moment the room was hushed. Then Operator 5 directed softly. "Back against the wall, Commander."

He broke off abruptly as ringing footfalls sounded on the deck outside, and sidestepped swiftly to the door. His darting hand shot a bolt into its socket as the knob rattled.

A fist pounded at the frame. "What the devil! Open up, Clayton!"

Commander Walton shouted suddenly: "Captain Hunter! I'm being attacked by Operator 5! Guard that door! Seize him the instant he comes out!"

A startled exclamation came from outside. Captain Hunter bellowed orders and other men came running toward the door. Operator 5 heard them station themselves outside it, and his lips tightened. He moved again toward the radio equipment. Keeping his gun leveled at Commander Walton, his eyes burned into those of the radio operator.

"Now," he ordered quietly, "send that message!"

Commander Walton said to the radio man. "You may use the key, Clayton. I think you understand."

"Yes, sir!"

OPERATOR 5 listened intently as the wireless expert reached for the sending key, and began to click it. His glance at the dials and switches assured him that the dots and dashes were actually flashing through the ether. He heard the clicks of the signal call to General Staff; he heard the first two words of the message tapped out, and then his hand shot swiftly to the sender's wrist.

"Back up!" he commanded.

With the startled operator standing at the steel wall beside Commander Walton, Operator 5 turned, and brought his own hand to the sending key. A wry smile tightened his lips.

"You were about to inform General Staff," he said to Clayton softly, "that I am holding the Commander at the point of a gun. "I am quite familiar, you see, with both codes."

Admiral Walton smiled sneeringly. "After this episode, Operator 5," he challenged, "you'll find yourself cashiered out of the service and quite familiar with the interior of a Federal prison."

"I'm obliged to admit," Operator 5 answered tightly, "that perhaps you're right."

His fingers worked the key as he spoke. Into the ether, from the battle-torn air of the Pacific area, his message flashed, directed to General Staff of the War Department in Washington, D.C.

He was aware, as he sent it, that it was one of the most startling messages ever addressed to them. And when the last word was finished, the radio operator blurted:

"God, sir! Do you know what he's asking. He wants General Staff to—"

"Suppose," Operator 5 cut in quietly, "we wait to see if General Staff will grant my unusual request."

Suddenly hard knuckles rapped again on the door. The voice of Captain Hunter called in huskily.

"Commander! The *Northampton's* trying to cut out of formation—she's shining like the others, sir! She's going in another second. She's so close that she'll—"

There was the sound of a terrific blast. The concussion struck numbness into the ears of these within the steel walls of the *Oklahoma's* radio room, even. Then, unseen by them, presaged only by the warning shouts of others on deck, the flagship rocked in a violent swell as sizzling, ragged pieces of metal hurtled from the air and clanged on the deck. For long moments the great boat pitched as if in torment while the effects of the explosion churned the sea.

"The *Northampton*, sir," Operator 5 said quietly, his eyes on Admiral Walton, "has been destroyed."

AGAIN KNUCKLES rapped the door Operator 5 ignored the sound and affixed the earphones on his head, still keeping the automatic leveled on the two men backed to the wall. Deftly he adjusted the sensitive equipment and, stepping aside, gestured toward a pair of auxiliary phones lying on the table.

"Use them, Clayton," he directed. "Transcribe the message when it comes in."

Clayton, his eyes on the gun, came forward and slipped on the phones.

Operator 5's nerves tightened during the interval. His request was so extraordinary, he knew, that its chances of being flatly refused were far greater than of its being granted.

"It's coming in!" Clayton blurted. "Message coming in from General Staff!" Operator 5 said quietly. "Transcribe it, Clayton. We'll check each other." He stood motionless, gun still on the Commander, while the amazed radio operator's pencil flew.

"You may be astounded to learn, Commander," Jimmy Christopher said quietly, "that the chief of operations of the Yellow Squadron doubtless considers that you, and not he, has struck the first blow in the new war!"

Clayton's pencil sputtered and stopped. He jerked up, and Operator 5 took the crisp message from his hand.

The scrawled lines brought a bright, keen light into his eyes. Immediately he slipped his gun into its holster, a tight smile curving his lips.

The instant the weapon vanished, Commander Walton took swift strides toward the bolted door, snapped it open, and three officers lurched into the room, guns in hands. They stopped short, leveling the weapons full upon Jimmy Christopher. He faced them with shoulders squared, looking each over quizzically.

"Lower your guns, gentlemen! Those are orders from your Commander!"

Admiral Walton sneered. "Commander? You're under arrest, and *my* orders are that you'll be held prisoner aboard this ship!"

"Your orders. Admiral Walton," Operator 5 answered easily, "are no longer effective aboard the *Oklahoma*. You have forced me to take this drastic step. Read, sir, this dispatch from General Staff."

Admiral Walton snatched the proffered message, read—and his face went deathly pale. Over his shoulders the officers peered, after which they too looked stunned. The message read:

SPECIAL ORDERS, REAR-ADMIRAL WALTON IS HEREWITH DEMOTED TO THE RANK OF LIEUT. COMMANDER, EFFECTIVE AT ONCE.

OPERATOR 5 IS HEREWITH APPOINTED COMMANDER OF THE US PACIFIC FLEET EFFECTIVE AT ONCE.

ORDERS NOW BEING DISPATCHED TO COMMANDERS OF THE PACIFIC LINE TO EXECUTE ORDERS OF OPERATOR 5 WITHOUT QUESTION.

BY ORDER MAJOR-GENERAL FALK, CHIEF OF STAFF.

THEY RAISED dazed eyes to those of Operator 5. He spoke quietly, firmly. "You have your orders, gentlemen. Lower your guns!"

The bewildered officers slowly obeyed. His fiery gaze jerked them to attention, and they snapped salutes. He spoke quietly again, through the thunderous roar beating across the sea.

"Transmit orders at once to all Commanders of the line to cease firing. Order all ships to withdraw eastward, in good order and under full steam. We are to proceed at once toward San Diego Bay!"

The men could not move.

"I trust, gentlemen," Operator 5 added softly, "that I shall not be obliged to offer charges of insubordination and mutiny against you."

The men grew pale. Rear-Admiral Walton flinched at the word. The air reverberated again with the thunder of big guns; and the roar jerked the men into action. Admiral Walton strode stiffly to the radio table and Operator 5, hurrying now to the door, heard him snap directions to carry out the orders to withdraw. Grimly Jimmy Christopher, with Tim Donovan at his heels, climbed to the bridge of the flagship.

When Diane Elliot hurried to his side he exclaimed: "Thank God, General Staff gave me power to lead the fleet out of this trap!"

He stood by, watching his orders being carried out. Under the thick darkness of night, the great gray warriors of the deep were beginning to swing heavily, executing a maneuver that sent them plunging through the swells toward the east.

The big guns had grown silent. The searchlights of the fleet were blinking out. Overhead airplanes roared still—forced to remain in the air because their carrier had plunged to the bottom. Jimmy Christopher checked the compass, made sure the fleet was proceeding strictly in accordance with his orders, and turned briskly as Captain Hunter strode to the bridge.

"An air observer has reported that the Yellow Squadron is steaming after us, sir, with the troop transports following! They will follow us into the Bay—certainly begin their invasion!"

"The Yellow invasion," Jimmy Christopher answered tightly, "is a certainty anyway. No move we can make will stop it now.

TIM DONOVAN

We can only hope to preserve our remaining ships. My orders stand!"

He ducked out into the tearing wind and lashing spray, to peer at the great ships plunging across the black sea. The sea frothed behind them as their engines exerted every possible ounce of power; their stems were cleaving the swells at top speed. Bringing binoculars to his eyes, Operator 5 turned the circles of his vision from one to another of the ships, alert for the first new evidence of that strange, hotly destructful power.

Suddenly he saw a glow creep along the antenna wires of the ship now last in the formation, the light cruiser *Concord*. Along the filaments the shine played, brightening quickly. Every nerve alert, Jimmy Christopher watched it. He scarcely heard when an officer came to a breathless stop behind him and gasped:

"*Concord* reports intense heat aboard, sir!"

JIMMY CHRISTOPHER watched, as the glow of the *Concord's* aerial wires brightened, then dulled, then brightened again. He saw fumes rising from the heights of the superstructure as the gray paint blistered; though no smoke rose from any lower point.

As if striving her utmost to escape the invisible power, the cruiser hurled through the rolling sea with her funnels pouring black. Bit by bit she forged ahead of the line, her paint still fuming, but freeing herself of the creeping force of destruction. At last, as Jimmy Christopher still watched, the final flickers of that fearsome shine disappeared.

Lieut. Commander Hall advanced to Operator 5 grimly. "The *Concord* reports that the heat is diminishing, sir!"

"We are moving beyond the reach of that power, in spite of the fact that the Yellow Squadron is following us under full steam. My orders still—"

Crashing reverberations thundered in the distance. The flare of big guns lighted the sky beyond the western horizon.

Operator 5 whipped about, peered out to where the ominous Yellow Fleet lay, saw again the glare of big guns, flinging out their projectiles. Overhead, giant shells passed, moaning away to the east. After which, from far beyond the horizon, at some point along the California shore, new thunder rumbled as the shells struck.

"Bombardment! The Yellow Fleet is beginning a bombardment of the coast!"

The nimble fingers of Operator 5 strayed slowly to the golden death-charm on his watch-chain. "The first step," he said in almost a whisper, "of the Yellow invasion of the United States."

CHAPTER 3
THE SAFFRON TERROR

THE SKY dropped doom. Along the western coast of the nation, destruction reared up, crested with death and terror.

Shells shrieked out of the ocean night, upon Los Angeles. The dull thunder of big guns firing far away had rumbled a warning across the city; and now the full fury of a storm of war struck down. Into the main business section tons of explosive plunged.

Flame sheeted high in Pershing Square, lighting falling

masonry, flickering over scattering, horrified crowds. Thousands ran madly from theaters, restaurants, night-clubs. Rending concussions ripped along Wilshire Boulevard, tossing cars about like toys. Projectiles howled into Griffith Park; the tall City Hall trembled on its foundations as a shell struck its front, crashed stone down, laid the skeleton of steel bare. And as the shocking reverberations echoed a note of doom over the "City of Angels" the snarling of airplanes came into the sky.

Swooping above the Hollywood reservoir, Yellow battle planes dropped gleaming bombs which, in striking the water, burst and spewed some viscid amber stuff over the whipping surface. Germ cultures! The new war with bacteria! Into the reservoir penetrated the deadly power of typhoid.

Whirling above Westlake Park, other Yellow airplanes sent vaned bombs spinning down to the green. Hollow explosions sounded like mocking laughter. Into the surrounding streets spread sticky, pungent fumes. The invisible power of lethal gas crept through the air.

The deadly Green Cross crushed men and women strangling to the sidewalks, burning into their lungs, drowning them in their own blood. Over the broad thoroughfares Death Dew rained, seeping into homes and stores, striking those who had no protection from it. Lewisite spewed from the sky, reaching down foggy fingers that brought death the instant they touched. The wings of the Yellow air fleet whipped doom and destruction through the air.

Into residential districts bombs plunged to burst with fiery violence. Spattering thermite, burning as it flew, carried fire throughout the city. Flames spread from home to home until whole blocks, whole sections became engulfed. Through the business district, buildings became roaring shells as the consuming thermite ate its way from roofs to basements. Scores of great blazes flicked into the sky—beacon fires of doom.

From every air base along the western coast, Army and Navy planes sprang into the sky to combat the Yellow warbirds. The beating of motors in the air became a rising turmoil. Along the coast, all defense batteries went into action, hurling shell upon shell out into the ocean. All along the sea line from San Diego to Seattle, the defense forces of the United States rose to combat the threatened Yellow invasion. But they fought only with guns—while the Yellow forces turned upon them not only guns but weapons they could not see, weapons that swiftly spread havoc. And one more terrible than all.

AT THE Naval Training Station at San Diego, snarling birds of war perched on the field, trembling with power as their props whipped over, straining to leap into the air battle—and this mysterious power struck. An oppressive heat circulated through the air. Officers, pilots, ground crew, all felt a stifling fever creep through their bodies. They heard the crackling of metal growing hot—and saw, all over the air base, the warning glow of the dread power manifesting itself.

Airplanes on the ground swiftly became shining things with blistering wings, with bubbling tires, with props throwing off sparks like gigantic pinwheels! Desperately pilots leaped from their pits—to find themselves surrounded by sizzling heat. Crazily, men tore off their uniforms, striving to free themselves of bits of metal now sparkling hot. And suddenly a furor of explosions shook the field.

Planes burst with shattering concussions as the fuel in their hot tanks ignited. Wings flew off, fuselages ripped apart, propellers spun free of their bosses. Hangars became ovens and inside them other crates crashed asunder.

Great guns barked at the coast battery near Los Angeles. Cannon recoiled, crews rushed to reload. And suddenly, as cradles carried silken bags of high-explosive to the breeches, a startled paralysis stopped the men. Again the dread, swift heat began to creep into the air—heat that fevered their bodies, began to radiate from the glistening barrels, mounted swiftly to withering intensity.

Swift seconds brought a glow of red heat to the big guns. Silk smoked on the crackling cradles as men fled in terror. Swift seconds—and the blow descended: high-explosive roared out its power, magazines burst with a violence that sent tremors through the earth and along the shore. At one moment the powerful battery had been barking its defiance at the Yellow Squadron steaming offshore; in the next it had vanished, leaving only a raw smoking hollow in the earth to mark its one-time location.

Up and down the west coast the invisible terror played. Huge tanks of illuminating gas grew red hot and burst. Powder magazines splintered the earth beneath them as they blew up. Ammunition exploded before it could be placed into guns. Weapons became too hot to touch. Everything combustible caught the spreading flames of havoc.

Seattle felt the shock of falling shells, San Francisco trembled with terrific concussions, Los Angeles rocked as the full force of the bombardment fell upon her, San Diego shuddered as the Naval base vanished off the face of the earth—the grisly red terror lighted the whole western sky.

High-explosive shells! Deadly bacteria! Poison gasses! Spattering, flaming thermite! Heat that came out of nowhere, suffocating and blistering and consuming all it touched....These the weapons of the Yellow Empire, played upon the western coast, opening the way for the saffron flood of invasion!

THE LIGHT of flickering flames played over a remote section of Los Angeles, as a swift car swerved to the curb in front of a small building conspicuous in no respect. Its brakes slapped it to a stop, and Operator 5 slipped from the wheel. He stood alert in the wavering light, senses sharpened, peering about.

His orders had sent the decimated Pacific Fleet plowing southward, out of the field of action. It lay beyond San Diego Bay now, beyond the range of the invisible sweep of the heat force. Operator 5's orders, as specially appointed Commander, were keeping the big guns silent so that the position of the ships might not be betrayed to the destructive onslaught. He had boarded a plane of the *Oklahoma;* a catapult had shot it into the night at a speed of sixty miles an hour; and swiftly he had piloted it to Glendale Airport.

He noted, as he stood in the dark in front of the inconspicuous building, that the sea wind was carrying the lethal gas inland. Murky clouds of it were rolling toward the mountains.

Buildings were flaming all around. Still bodies lay in the streets beyond, shrouded by the light.

Grimly Operator 5 signaled, and Tim Donovan drove the car nearer. He leaned into it, removing a small silver case from his pocket, and spoke to Diane Elliot.

"Drive, Di! Head east and make the fastest time possible! Using a plane now is too dangerous, but you've got to get your-

THE MYSTERY YACHT

self beyond the area of invasion tonight. Take these—use them. They'll counteract any poison gas."

The girl took two small, porcelain ovals from the silver case. She knew that they were of Operator 5's own devising, impregnated with a preparation he had compounded. Inserted into the nostrils, they functioned as an aspirator.

Her eyes pleaded with his as she shifted to the wheel.

"Jimmy, what are you going to do? It will be fatal to stay here in the west! Jimmy, are you sure of what you've done—ordering the fleet to retreat and—"

"I'm taking the full responsibility for that action, Di. I'm convinced that any other move would have meant even worse losses for us. Now step on it! Get back as fast as you can drive—and wait for word from me!"

He moved back as the girl sent the car spurting away. His darkened gaze followed as she swung through the flickering light of the flames, heading east. As the car sped from sight, he stepped to the door of the inconspicuous, lightless building, Tim Donovan at his side.

He rapped—peculiarly. A bolt clicked, and he stepped into darkness. Tim Donovan came beside him as the voice of an unseen man asked: "You wish a treatment?"

"I have an appointment for five."

The blurted answer was: "The chief has been waiting for word from you!"

Jimmy Christopher seized Tim Donovan by the arm, led the boy along the lightless hallway. At a rear entrance he carefully drew the bolt. His instructions were a whisper:

"Stay out there, old timer, and out of sight. "You'll need two of these aspirators—take them! It's certain the Yellow Empire has been operating an espionage office in this section, and they may have this place under observation. Keep your eyes open boy, and wait for me!"

"Sure, Jimmy." Tim exclaimed. "You can depend on me!"

"I know I can, old-timer—for anything."

The door opened, closed quietly; the tough little Irish lad slipped out. Operator 5 turned back. Pausing at another door, he knocked again. His signal brought a metallic click—an electrical lock being released. He pushed into a dark room, crossed it, opened a door, and stepped into a brightly lighted office.

IT WAS walled with file cabinets, and there were no windows. A breathy sound in the air indicated that a ventilating system was in operation, clarifying the air of all lethal gasses as it pumped. The frantic clatter of teletype machines echoed from an adjoining room. The air was charged with an electrical tension in these hidden offices—secret headquarters LA, of the United States Intelligence Service.

A white headed man came swiftly from behind the desk and gripped the hand of Operator 5. He was V-3, chief of the LA office, acting under the orders of the central headquarters in Washington, D.C.

"I received your wireless message from the *Oklahoma*, that you were coming, Operator 5!" he exclaimed huskily. "WDC-13 is clamoring for word from you. Fortunately, the wires are still open. But at any moment a shell may break them, or Yellow espionage agents find and cut them. For God's sake, report to Z-7 at once."

Jimmy Christopher stepped briskly into the adjoining communications room. In a row of booths the teletype machines were clicking out curling yellow tape blackened with automatically deciphered code messages. Two wireless experts frantically handled dispatches before their sensitive shortwave equipment. At a switchboard a telephone operator made and broke connections with dizzy speed. To him Operator 5 spoke crisply, then stepped into a soundproof booth in the corner of the room.

Clicks sounded on the wire as his connections went through, opening a secret line from coast to coast linking him directly with central headquarters WDC-13 in Washington. The voices of intermediate operators echoed; and abruptly a deep-chested tone carried over the wire.

Z-7, chief of all United States Intelligence activities, known by no other designation even to his most trusted agents, was speaking.

"Operator 5, I have orders of the utmost urgency for you! I've a full report of the bombardment and impending invasion, and it's certain, now, we can do nothing to stop the invasion. But it's absolutely necessary to us to maintain our undercover organization in Los Angeles!"

"Yes, Chief!"

"You will doubtless be forced to abandon the present offices. In that or any other event, our operators must be held together. Somehow a new base of communications must be established for them. Somehow you must keep us in touch with that point. It is a highly important job, and I am delegating it to you. It is your responsibility to maintain LA somehow and to keep a line of communication open between it and WDC-13."

"I understand, Chief!"

"Unless we are able to maintain LA, as well as other headquarters in the west, we will be struck absolutely blind—working under a simply insurmountable handicap in our attempts to repel this damnable invasion."

OPERATOR 5 spoke briskly. "What steps are being taken, Chief?"

"The Army is being mobilized and sent into that quarter with all possible speed. The Navy cannot combat the invasion once it begins; that must be left to the military."

"Chief!" Jimmy Christopher explained. "Is that the decision of General Staff?"

"It is! No one department of our defense can hope to cope with the situation. The Navy is—by itself—helpless. The Air Corps can only cooperate with other units. The weight of the task rests upon the Army!"

"Chief!" Operator 5's voice crackled in protest. "Isn't General Staff aware that the Yellow forces are using a new weapon against us—a weapon we are totally unable to defend ourselves from?"

"I know, my boy! I have reports from all air bases and coast defense units. Almost all of them have been wiped out. Whatever that damnable power is, it's rendered us almost helpless in the face of the coming invasion. We have neither planes nor cannon in the west to use against the Yellow forces now. What's worse, most of our ammunition stores have been exploded by this same force. General Staff is throwing the Army into that area, and sending the Atlantic Fleet into the Pacific, in order to—"

"Wait!" Jimmy Christopher interrupted ringingly. "Doesn't General Staff realize that moving the Army into this area will mean even worse disaster? It will not stop the invasion! It will open the way for the Yellowese to move unhampered—to sweep across the entire nation to the east!"

"The decision of the General Staff is made."

"It must be changed, Chief—at all costs!"

"The move is being carried out now, my boy!"

"Then it must be stopped! It must!"

Z-7's blurted retort came after a bewildered pause. "Can you possibly mean you believe we should make no move whatsoever to repulse the Yellow invasion?"

"I mean exactly that, Chief! I insist that we must preserve our defensive forces—not squander them before a power we cannot hope to combat!"

Z-7's voice became edged. "My boy, the armed defense of the nation is not under the command of the Intelligence. Our work is mapped out for us. *Your* job is to maintain, at all costs, the LA organization in the west!"

"Chief!" Operator 5 implored. "You've got to listen to me! You've got to do everything possible to influence General Staff from deliberately—"

"You have your orders, Operator 5!"

The sharp rebuke stung Jimmy Christopher as the connection broke. Slipping out of the soundproofed booth he strode to the desk of V-3. His face was pale, his eyes glittering, as he swiftly read reports scattered on the desk—reports that gave an appalling record of Yellow destruction.

Air fields wiped out. Coast defense units blown off the face of the earth. Cities disrupted by that invisible heat from hell. Devastation wrought along a mighty seacoast, from northern border to southern!

HE STOOD quietly, while V-3 eyed him. He scarcely heard the white haired sub-chief say:

"Z-7 informed me that he would issue orders to you for the continuance of this organization after the invasion. I recommended this myself. It is a highly important job, one demanding the cleverest strategy. You are equal to it—I fear I am not. Have you orders for me, Operator 5?"

Jimmy Christopher's eyes darkened. Whispered words came from his lips.

"Long ago—perhaps—this new weapon was first turned upon us. An experiment then—perhaps. The *Fulton* may have been a warning—a warning we did not heed. It's too late now!" *

V-3 stepped closer, his face lined deep with anxiety. The sharpness of his voice aroused Operator 5.

"We must take steps at once to preserve this organization against the invasion. Have you orders?"

* AUTHOR'S NOTE: The United States Navy gunboat *Fulton,* on March 14, 1934, with 194 officers and men aboard, while on patrol duty in Bias Bay on the north coast of Hong Kong, was destroyed by flames.

The cause of the fire was not immediately known, although it was reported that an explosion occurred. The disaster took place in a heavy fog in the bay, which has frequently been the scene of naval operations by the British and the United States. Rear Admiral Frank C. Upham, Commander of the United States Asiatic Fleet, wirelessed to the Navy Department a report that the *Fulton* was burning furiously when other vessels went to her aid and succeeded in rescuing all aboard.

The United States maintains two gunboat patrols in China, one on the Yangtze River from Shanghai to the Yangtze gorges above Hankow, the other on the Pearl River, between Hong Kong and Canton. Both patrols are permitted under Chinese-American treaties. Bias Bay, where the *Fulton* met disaster, is one of the most notorious pirate strongholds in the world. Scores of ships, including large ocean-going vessels, have been seized by Chinese pirates and looted there.

Jimmy Christopher's lips tightened in a mirthless smile; his tone was that of a man whose determination cannot be shaken.

"You know Z-7's information. *You* will carry it out, V-3—not I! If there is still a whole plane on Glendale field, I'm going to take it now—for Washington."

V-3 stared. "Can you mean you're deliberately refusing to act on Z-7's orders?"

Jimmy Christopher's words clicked. "Preserving this undercover organization is important; but to save the Army from utter annihilation is far more important! Neither this headquarters nor any other will be of the slightest use once the Yellow forces seize control of the nation. *That's* what we're facing! That's why I'm disregarding the chief's orders and flying to Washington!"

Briskly Operator 5 turned from the inner office. He stepped into the dark corridor and strode to the rear entrance. With the door closed behind him, he stood at the edge of an open space across which the wavering light of flames played. Overhead Yellow planes, the carriers of the doom which had struck Los Angeles, still droned.

He stepped alertly along the rear wall of the building. "Tim!" he called. When no answer came, his eyes sharpened, swiftly searched the gloom.

"Tim!" He sprang anxiously to the corner of the building. But as he came in sight of the littered street, he stopped short.

The shadowed figure of a man showed near the building, beside a heavy car drawn up to the curb. The man stood erect, at his shoulder a weapon which appeared to be a rifle, with a grotesquely thick barrel and a spherical object affixed to its muzzle.

The dark figure was aiming directly at the wall of the building. Instantly Operator 5 acted.

His automatic flashed into his hand. A flick of the trigger snapped a bullet through the air an instant after the strange rifle exploded, with a muffled concussion.

The recoil of the thick barreled weapon jolted the shadowy figure backward. Simultaneously, a sharp crushing sound came from the wall of the building, a black, splintered hole appeared and from inside sounded a booming explosion.

The man with the rifle whirled back. Operator 5 leaped after him, sending one sharp glance into the car as he ran. Its rear door sagged open and the light of the flames, playing inside, disclosed a small, still figure sprawled on the mat—a boy, Tim Donovan. Operator 5's heart flashed cold at the sight.

THE MAN with the rifle whirled behind the car and he heard the click of a shell sliding into the chamber of the weird weapon, saw the black figure shove a rod down its bore on the end of which a black ball was affixed. The thing was swung toward him—while, above it, gleaming eyes gazed along the barrel. Jimmy Christopher swiftly sprang nearer, used his right to click loose the buckle of his belt. He jerked it from its loops, and a glittering rapier leaped in his hand. His first swift slash caught the other's upraised arm, and stinging steel brought paralysis to the finger even then pressing the trigger.

A howl of wrath tore from the lips of the man and, as he

lurched back, the rifle dropped from his hands. Then Jimmy Christopher had his gleaming blade poised at the other's heart.

"Stay where you are!" He kicked the rifle out of reach. "Back—steady!"

Inside the secret headquarters building he heard muffled shouts, saw the entrance burst open and men rush through in terror. Behind them shone the bright glare of flames. The roar of an intense fire carried out as dispatchers and secret agents rushed into the open. With them hurried V-3, face white as death, shouting dismayed orders.

"Abandon the building!"

Jimmy Christopher kept his rapier poised, glancing down at the queer rifle. He realized that its power had fired a charge of combustible through the wall—perhaps thermite. He knew that the weapon had sent destruction into the very midst of the hidden headquarters. The roaring flames inside the building meant the complete disruption of communications with WDC-13, paralysis of the undercover system in Los Angeles. His jaw muscles bunched hard as he peered at the man backed against the car.

"You're an agent of the Yellow espionage office," he declared softly, "or perhaps—"

A terrified light sprang into the eyes of the captive; with a quick, desperate sweep of his arm he attempted to thrust the rapier aside. The keen edge itself frustrated the attack; the steel granted on bared bone. With a maddened lurch, the man tried to strike. Operator 5 did not move; but he felt the steel of his rapier tremble. A gasp broke from the other's lips as he peered down in chilled amazement—at the strand of steel which his own move had driven deep into his body. With a strangled moan he folded to his knees, melted in the flickering light.

Operator 5 stepped back, his *épée* gleaming red. He spun past the car, glimpsed flames roaring out of the open door of LA, saw secret agents scattering in the gloom. Then he ducked into the car and seized Tim Donovan's shoulders. The boy was just recovering consciousness—and squirming with pain.

"Tim! Tim, old-timer!"

The tough little Irish lad tried to struggle up, touched a cruel welt on his forehead, blinked through blood which had trickled into his eyes, then gripping Operator 5's hand tightly, climbed to his knees.

"I'm all right, Jimmy. Gee, I tried to stop him, but he—"

"Steady, boy! Get into the front seat! We've got to move!"

As the youth staggered up, Jimmy Christopher circled to the espionage agent lying dead on the littered pavement. Jerking off the man's hat, he peered in amazement at the face revealed in the light These were not the features of a Yellowese, but of an American!

Searching the dead man's clothing, he detected one cunningly hidden pocket behind the lapel, drew a thread to open it, and brought a bright circle of gleaming copper metal into his palm. On one side it bore the numeral 27; on the other, 2700X-W.

He dropped it into his pocket and slid beneath the wheel of the secret agent's car. Withering heat beat upon him while the starter ground. The building that had housed headquarters LA was a roaring furnace, its walls corroding before the swift acid of the flames.

As the car spurted away, Operator 5 said to Tim, grimly: "It's only a matter of hours until our western coast will be occupied by the armed forces of the Yellow Emperor!"

CHAPTER 4
THE VOICE OF TREASON

O UT OF the west and across the United States, electrical impulses vibrated to make the ether a chaos. The great broadcasting chains of the country, attempting to inform a terrorized people of the Yellow threat swooping across the Pacific, fought impossible barriers. Millions of radio listeners, attempting to tune in their nearest stations, heard only a deafening crackle and sputter. Over the entire dial spread a roar that drowned out all broadcasting.

Deliberately, from the Yellow ships riding off the western coast, the powerful impulses were being shot into the ether in order to prevent the American people hearing the reassurances of the government's spokesmen, in order to break their morale with a terrifying uncertainty.

Newspapers remained the swiftest means of spreading the news of the attack upon the United States—and newspapers streamed from roaring presses. Gigantic headlines carried appalling information.

YELLOW TROOPS OCCUPYING CALIFORNIA!

INVASION OF THE YELLOW WARLORDS

ENEMY LINES ADVANCING EASTWARD!
ARMY RUSHED WEST TO COMBAT INVADERS!

Among the startling dispatches which drove terror into the hearts of millions were those telling how the Yellow power was striking even at this means of news-distribution.

NEWSPAPERS BOMBED!
KEY CITIES REPORT SABOTAGE!
PARK ROW, NEW YORK, WRECKED BY BLASTS!

Battling myriad handicaps, the staffs of those newspaper offices which remained untouched labored to carry heartening information to the people.

ARMY SPEEDING WEST AGAINST YELLOW LINE!
ATLANTIC FLEET STEAMING THROUGH CANAL!
NATION'S DEFENSES MOBILIZED IN WEST!

Men and women, horrified by the Yellow invaders, had little thought for foreign dispatches which stated that war was spreading through the entire panorama of the Far East, that, in particular, Russia was mobilizing her scanty sea power in a hasty attempt to protect her Asiatic territory. Reminders that preparations for war had been under way for many months meant nothing now, for the actual war was striking at this very moment at the vitals of the United States.

The Yellow invasion was a terrifying actuality. Yellow hordes had already swarmed across the coast. Yellow commanders already ruled the ports and key cities of the western states.

CARTER CASE

Yellow forces, off scores of ships, carrying armaments with them, were even now driving eastward. A Yellow scourge had spread upon the land an ulcerous, deadly growth which threatened annihilation to the entire nation.

In Washington, D.C., the tension of the crisis tightened swiftly. Stunned astonishment was succeeded by alert counter-action. Orders flashed, marshalling the defensive forces of the nation; information echoed back, painting the cataclysmic danger which loomed.

ATLANTIC FLEET TO BACK PACIFIC—ON WAY!

GENERAL BALTA

FULL ARMY STRENGTH BEING THROWN INTO
WEST! YELLOW LINE ADVANCES INLAND AND
STOPS! HALT OF YELLOW FORCES SHROUDED
IN MYSTERY!

AS THE sinister developments brought fresh anxiety to the
people, as reassurance was balanced by heavier uncertainty, a
handful of men at the hub of the nation gravely considered the
tactical problem of the Yellow invasion.

The Joint Board—otherwise called the General Staff—of the
Army and Navy of the United States was in historic conference.

In a vaulted room in the building of the Department of War,
these firm-eyed commanders of the nation's defenses faced each
other in the crisis, not one daring to voice the fear gnawing at his
heart; each attempting to appear confident in the face of tragic
uncertainty, each concealing his self-recrimination because due
preparations had not long ago been made against the threat of
the very catastrophe which now faced them.

Theirs was the pressing necessity of stemming the Yellow
tide of reclaiming the west for the United States. Theirs was the
staggering task of repulsing the Yellow hordes.

They regarded each other in grave silence as they sat
around the conference table. Major-General Falk, Chief of
Staff. Major-General Mortman, Deputy Chief of Staff. Brigadier-General Hartwell, Assistant Chief of Staff, War Plans
Division. Admiral Frankson, Chief of the Bureau of Aeronau-
tics, Navy. Rear-Admiral Monroe, Chief of Naval Operations.
Rear-Admiral Gordon, Director of War Plans Division. Captain

Jarrell, Representative of War Plans Division, Office of Naval Operation.

With them sat members of the President's Cabinet—the Secretaries of War and Navy. With them sat a man whose weapon against the enemy was secrecy—the commander-in-chief of the United States Intelligence Service, known as Z-7.

Z-7's black eyes smoldered as the commanders of the nation's defenses conferred.

"Gentlemen," Major-General Falk addressed his colleagues. "Had the United States, long ago, taken due heed of the danger lying in the Pacific, as Russia has done, we might now be spared this emergency. We did not. It is too late for regrets. There remains only to fight—to fight to our utmost. I think we are agreed, gentlemen, that we have ordered the only possible move—the mobilization and shift of our Army into the zone of war."

A knock sounded at the door. The Secretary of the Joint Board rose quickly. As he answered the summons, the Chief of Staff continued.

"Perhaps it is this move of ours—our throwing of our entire Army into the West—which has brought the advance of the Yellow line to its first abrupt check. There's no topographical reason for their sudden halt. The mountains are no real barrier to them. Nor have they paused because they're content with the coast region they've already claimed. They've stopped, gentlemen, to dig in and fight our advancing Army!"

The Secretary turned in surprise from the door, closed it, stepped to Z-7 and whispered.

"This, gentlemen," the Chief of Staff continued, "gives us confidence. Our Army can repulse the invasion, and it will. We are superior in numbers. We are superior in equipment. We are thoroughly familiar with the terrain. I believe, gentlemen, that once our Army strikes, the Yellow danger will be ended—the invaders wiped out, the West Coast again under our control."

Z-7 had come slowly to his feet. The information whispered to him by the Secretary had taken the color from his face, brightened the fiery light in his eyes. Now, as Major-General Falk paused, he leaned forward to speak.

"Gentlemen, Operator 5 is here."

The Chief of Staff stiffened. "Here? That young man *here?*"

"He's just outside that door. He has just come from the Pacific Coast by plane. He wishes to be allowed to speak to the members of the General Staff."

THE OFFICERS of the Joint Board peered sternly at Z-7. He winced inwardly, sensing the hostility they now felt toward the young man known as Operator 5. His own bewilderment contributed to the moment of torture he experienced. Presently, his voice frosty, Major-General Falk answered:

"Let him come in."

Z-7 stepped to the door, opened it, and Operator 5 strode briskly into the room. His cheeks were haggard; his features lined with fatigue; his movements those of a man who, almost at the point of exhaustion, forces himself on; yet his eyes were brilliantly alight. He paused just inside the door as Z-7 spoke huskily.

"Operator 5, I issued you strict orders to remain in the west in order to maintain the organizations of our LA men."

"I know I've violated your orders, Chief," Jimmy Christopher answered tightly, "by coming here."

He strode to the conference table, the cold eyes of the officers still fixed on him, and gazed from one stern face to another. He placed his palms on the table and leaned forward. When he spoke, his voice rang with the resonance of indomitable conviction.

"While I stood outside that door, I could not help overhearing your statement, General Falk. I heard you express your belief that the Yellow line has stopped its advance because it fears our superior strength. I heard you declare your confidence that our Army will have no difficulty in driving the invaders out.

"Allow me to say, gentlemen, that I realize my office of service is a small one. I possess no authority whatever in any branch of the government, and you men are able to issue orders which carry the strength of law. I ask only that you listen to me explain why I am convinced that you are making a tragic mistake—a mistake that may be the cause of the annihilation of the United States."

A chill silence followed his words. The hostility in the eyes of the officers became more pronounced. Major-General Falk's voice grated as he declared slowly:

"Young man, I warn you that this board entertains grave doubts as to the wisdom of your move in commanding the withdrawal of the Pacific Fleet. Every officer here keenly regrets our decision to grant you the power to make that move. We definitely feel, Operator 5, that the withdrawal of our fleet under your orders is the direct reason for the occupation of the West Coast by the Yellow forces at this precise minute!"

Jimmy Christopher's worn face paled. "You believe, gentlemen, that if I had not ordered that withdrawal, the invasion would not have taken place?"

"We are convinced of that!" Major-General Falk snapped. "We are convinced that if the blame for the initial success of the Yellow invasion—the blame for the razing of our cities, the destruction of our West Coast defenses, the deaths of thousands of enlisted men and civilians—if the blame for that can be fixed on any one man, it can be fixed on you!"

Operator 5 stood dazed. His unbelieving eyes shifted across the coldly stern glances of the General Staff. He turned to peer at Z-7—and in one swift stunning moment realized that the Washington chief was smitten with the same utter lack of understanding.

"It is only in view of your exemplary service to the nation in the past, my boy," Z-7 said quietly, "that we have not brought home to you the full consequences of your act."

"Chief! You can't possibly believe I deliberately opened the way for the Yellow invasion!"

"We have not brought ourselves to believe it was your purpose to do that," the Chief of Staff answered, ringingly. "But we are absolutely convinced that this tragedy is the direct result of an act of yours which—to say the very least—was unwise."

OPERATOR 5'S shoulder's squared "I will speak clearly, gentlemen. I ordered the withdrawal of the Pacific Fleet because its continued advance would have meant its total annihilation. I consider that my move has preserved, for our defense, ships which otherwise would now be resting on the bottom of the ocean. They are powerless at the moment, yes—but they are still able to fight. And the moment will come, I hope, when we can use them against the Yellowese on even terms. Right now the Yellowese still possess a terrific advantage over us—they still control a powerful force with which they can, if they wish, wipe this nation out of existence. The Yellow militarists *will* use that power to destroy us, gentlemen, if you persist in inviting them to do so!"

The lips of the Chief of Staff thinned. "If you understand the situation so thoroughly, Operator 5, perhaps you can explain to us the nature of this Yellow weapon."

"I cannot." Jimmy Christopher made the admission in a crackling voice. "I do not know what it is, but I know how it works. I have seen it strike utter destruction upon three great battleships—and what you know of it is based only on the reports you have received. Perhaps, gentlemen, you under-estimate that power. I believe you do. I believe it can be used to wipe the United States off the map, and I believe you are permitting that very objective in a way which is—to say the very least—unwise."

The officers of the General Staff stiffened in amazement as the bold irony of Operator 5's remark bit into them. When he resumed, he spoke into the coldness of unflinching enmity.

"The Yellow Command cannot intend to use such simple tactics as you believe. You overlook the fact that behind this invasion lie months and years of crafty planning. You have not taken into account the uncanny, merciless shrewdness of the oriental mind. The Yellow line has not 'dug in' because their leaders are afraid of our advancing Army. They're waiting for our Army to walk into the trap they have set—waiting to destroy it—waiting to swarm unhampered across this nation and seize it from coast to coast while we lie helpless!"

"And how," General Falk demanded with utter skepticism, "will they be enabled to destroy our Army and invade into the east?"

"They'll open the way with the same power that has crippled our Pacific fleet and destroyed our West Coast defenses. They'll spread annihilation into the east with exactly the same force that spread it along the thousands of square miles of our Pacific states."

"Of that we are utterly unconvinced!"

Again Operator 5 straightened. "Gentlemen! I stand discredited before you. You choose not to heed this warning. Heed it or not, I am bound to give it. Unwise or not, I am serving my country to the best of my ability. I will persist in serving it according to my convictions, regardless of all opposition, regardless of any consequences that may be meted out to me. I warn you, gentlemen, you must not continue the westward movement of our Army! You must recall all units at once! You must not advance to attack—you must retreat! Retreat, and we shall still have an army with which to fight! Advance, and you will see it wiped out of existence before your very eyes!"

"We advance!"

A MOMENT of silence followed the thundering assertion of the Chief of Staff. The face of Operator 5 grew deathly white. His hands closed into fists; his eyes became black. Then ignoring the gesture of dismissal from the Chief of Staff, he again leaned forward tensely.

"Very well, gentlemen. Your orders are advancing the Army. I wish you to know, here and now, that I will do everything in my power to render your orders ineffective. If there is anything I can do to stop the march of our Army into utter oblivion—regardless of the consequences, gentlemen, I will do it!

"Good-night."

He spun on his heel, snapped out the door, and into the outer office. Tim Donovan had been waiting tensely, perched in a chair, and now the staunch little Irish lad hurried to his side. He sensed the turmoil in his friend's heart and his eyes expressed utter loyalty.

"I heard what you said, Jimmy," the boy declared quietly. "Gee, Jimmy—you know I'm with you!"

"Thanks, old timer," Operator 5 spoke softly. "At this moment, you're the only one in the world who's with me."

They turned as Z-7 came slowly from the conference room. The black eyes of the Washington chief searched the eyes of Operator 5. Lines of anxiety puckered his mouth, and his lips pressed hard before he said huskily: "I don't understand, my boy!"

"The General Staff does not realize, Chief, that this invasion is a crisis which cannot be handled according to stereotyped rules taught in a war college—during peace time."

"I do not understand, my boy," Z-7 repeated anxiously, "why

you have disobeyed my orders. I instructed you to maintain our LA men at all costs; but you abandoned the field. If any other had committed such an insubordination, I should not tolerate it an instant. But you—in the past you've given your country a noble service. It's not like you—"

"To the best of my ability, in the past, Chief, I have served this country. To the best of my ability now, I am serving it. Lord, Chief! Do you doubt me too?"

"Immediately after I telephoned you your orders," Z-7 said with quiet firmness, "LA was destroyed. One of my agents there managed to get word to me before the Yellow forces seized control of all communications. The destruction of that office made the execution of my orders ten times more necessary than before. Our men are scattered, and you should have stayed to reorganize them. You did not—and now we are helpless, blind as to the Yellow operations within that territory."

"I delegated that job to V-3, chief."

"V-3, my boy, is dead—dead of burns suffered in the fire which destroyed LA. All our other headquarters in the west are completely paralyzed. The service now has no point of communication in all the area held by the Yellow forces. We are left completely in the dark—because you disobeyed orders, because, when you might have saved our LA unit, you did not."

Operator 5 peered squarely into the smouldering eyes of Z-7. "My concern was not, and is not, for one small division of our service. "It's for our entire Army, our whole nation." He straightened. "Perhaps I have been—unwise. I say again that I am ready to accept the consequences...."

Z-7 frowned gravely. "Until now, General Staff has held you in the highest esteem. The events of the last hours have placed you in a dangerous position, Operator 5. I want you to vindicate yourself—and you can. We know only too well that the Yellowese are operating a tremendous spy ring in this country, that their espionage system has been built up to encircle the globe. The destruction of that system is our objective—is yours!"

"I pledge myself to do everything possible, Chief."

From his pocket Operator 5 drew the strange brass check, bearing the mysterious, stamped symbols. He studied it as the door opened and an Intelligence operator who had been waiting in the corridor stepped in to say: "The White House on the wire, Chief." Z-7 strode from the room, and Jimmy Christopher peered sharply at Tim Donovan.

"It was not a Yellowese who destroyed LA, but an American. We're fighting a secret force that we haven't even suspected until now, old timer… an American."

He turned smartly as Z-7 re-entered. The Washington chief's voice came sharp and clear.

"You are ordered to take part in an urgent conference with the President at the White House, Operator 5, in one hour."

CHAPTER 5
WEAPONS OF GOLD

OPERATOR 5 sent his roadster whirring along the road which flanked the Potomac. The swift car, part of the Intelligence fleet, was one which had awaited him at Bolling

Field in response to his radioed request, from his plane while in flight. Now, with Tim Donovan huddled at his side, he drove against time.

"Gee, Jimmy!" the boy exclaimed with deep concern. "You're getting yourself into serious trouble. Even Z-7 is turning against you."

"You'll never do that, will you, Tim? You'll never turn against me."

"Never, Jimmy! Gee, you know that!"

"Good boy! Yes, you're right—I've placed myself in an extremely precarious position. The worst of it is that I must, I absolutely must persist in it. Conscientiously it's impossible for me to do otherwise."

He turned off the highway sharply; followed a byroad; turned again, into the rear entrance of an estate which stood hard by the famous river. Clicking off the motor and turning out the lights, he strode to the gate in the high spiked fence, drew a key from his pocket, and unfastened the strong lock. Signaling Tim Donovan after him, he slipped through, then paused.

"What's this place, Jimmy?"

"An unoccupied estate that's been under litigation for years. I've prepared a retreat for myself here, Tim, in case of an emergency. No one else in the world knows about it but you—not even the chief. Follow me."

They trod through long grass toward a boathouse at the water's edge. It was a large structure, looming black against the night. Again Operator 5 unfastened a lock, stepped into thicker blackness. A moment of silence passed before he brought a small torch from his pocket and touched the button.

A narrow white beam shot across a stretch of water lapping inside the boat-house. Rocking gently there lay a trim white power-boat. A tarpaulin was half covering it, and Jimmy Christopher peered at it alertly. The beam of his light swung all around, probing into corners, then returned to the craft.

"I may be obliged to use this boat sometime soon, Tim," he declared. "I haven't been here for months; I've got to see that it's in tip-top condition."

The boy stood wide-eyed with surprise as Operator 5 swung into the boat, stooped, and opened the little hatch which housed the engine. Sloshing water covered its base; upon it floated a few fresh shavings of wood. Operator 5, now keenly wary, reached to a plug that protruded from a hole bored through the shell of the boat.

It was a metallic plug, driven home hard; yet it was so soft that flecks of the gray alloy came away on his fingernails. He poised in thought, then quickly examined the motor. He found it as he had left it, in prime condition. Quietly he rose, signaled the boy, and returned to the door. "It's all okay," he said. "We've got to be getting back to Washington right away."

He stepped out with Tim, closed the door, rattled the padlock in the hasp—but did not close it. Stepping back alertly, he stopped. Bending to the boy's ear, he whispered: "Get into the car, Tim! Start the motor and draw up the road a bit. Make it seem that we're leaving. Come back without a sound. There's somebody hiding in that boathouse now!"

THE STARTLED boy complied with alacrity, and while Operator 5 stood motionless in the gloom, the whirring of the car's motor sounded over the lapping of the waves along shore. Skillfully, Tim Donovan spurted up the road, playing the throttle to make it seem that the car was leaving the spot rapidly. In a moment he crept back, like a shadow, to Jimmy Christopher's side.

"Watch sharp, Tim! Somebody's found my boat—and tampered with it. A hole has been bored through the shell in the motor-housing, and plugged with alloy. The alloy will melt from the heat of the motor if that boat is sent out now. It would sink quickly. The man who did that job is certainly still in there."

"How do you know, Jimmy?"

"The hammer marks on the plug haven't had time to tarnish. The wood shavings aren't yet soaked with water. I heard a sound while we were in there—steady!"

He melted against the side of the boat-house, tugging the boy beside him. Some kind of movement had started at the edge of the water.

Up from the bank rose a shadow. It straightened, became the outline of a man—a man who had crept out of the boat-house at the broad doors, whose wet shoes made sticky noises now as he approached. He came slowly nearer—and paused.

Sharply Jimmy Christopher ordered, "Raise your hands, you—quickly!"

A flashing movement answered—a hand darting holsterward. Operator 5 made no move for his own weapon as he sprang forward. A gun glittered in the light as he darted aside.

Twice, swiftly, the weapon spat. Wood splintered beside Tim Donovan. Jimmy Christopher swung swiftly, feeling the slugs rip through his clothing, and struck with lightning swiftness.

His stiff fingers drove to the temple of the man with the gun. A sharp intake of breath resulted. The shadow-figure went rigid, and toppled like an unbalanced statue.

Jimmy Christopher caught him, lowered him to the grass, straightened and listened. Had the shots sounded an alarm—would the reports bring someone to the scene? Assured that his jiu-jitsu blow would render his assailant unconscious for the better part of an hour, he went on for prolonged moments, listening into undisturbed quiet.

"Tim!" he exclaimed then. "Are you all right, old-timer?"

"He almost got me, Jimmy!"

"Open the door!"

Operator 5 lifted the unconscious man easily, and carried him into the boathouse. When the door slapped to behind him he lowered the man and turned the white beam of his light on the mask-like face. In Los Angeles, attacking the espionage agent who had fired the secret headquarters, he had expected to find that the *saboteur* was a Yellowese and instead had found an American. Now, again, he stared in surprise into a face of unmistakable American characteristics.

Again he searched his man; again he found a secret pocket in the lapel; and from it removed a shining brass check. On its one side was stamped the numeral 33: on the other, 2700X-W.

He rose, peering as it glittered in the light.

"This side," he whispered, "is the same."

71

He turned quickly. While Tim Donovan held the light, he worked at a tool bench at one wall, deftly fashioning a wooden plug. Stepping into the boat, he tapped the metallic one from the hole in the shell. Water gushed in, and he instantly drove the wooden peg home. He straightened, and from a chest in one corner removed a coil of light rope. Carefully he bound the unconscious man. Then, signaling Tim Donovan after him, he stepped to the door.

"Another American—another Yellowese spy," he declared. "His intention was not to destroy the boat. He meant to have its passengers—you and I, Tim—drown when it took to deep water."

Again he glanced at the brass check, his eyes narrowing. Then, quickly, he stepped out and with Tim hurried to the car. Once at the wheel he sent it whirring in the direction of Washington.

He said nothing, though the boy searched his face with questioning eyes. Reaching the Capital, he turned into one of the radiating avenues, then turned again, and drove slowly past a corner, peering back at a dark building. Just beyond he swung to the curb and spoke quietly to Tim.

"This is X street. That building back there is 2700. I'm playing a chance that the designation on the brass checks is the address of a secret headquarters. The other side carries the mark of each spy. It may be a wrong lead, but—we've got to play it. Will you help, Tim?"

"Sure, Jimmy!"

"Keep an eye on that building, then. Watch anyone who enters. We don't dare make a false move. Look for the man we caught in the boathouse. I deliberately tied him so that he can get free easily. He may come here. It may not be soon, but once he shows up, I want to know of it right away. Call me at WDC-13, Tim."

"Sure, Jimmy!"

"On your toes, boy! I've got to go to the White House at once. I've just enough time to make it."

Tim Donovan slipped from the car, scurried along the sidewalk and melted into the darkness of a recessed doorway below the level of the street.

As he did so, Jimmy Christopher drove off—to keep his urgent conference with the President of the United States.

THE CHIEF of the White House detail of the Secret Service escorted Operator 5 from the entrance of the historic building to the door of the Chief Executive's study. Oil paintings of past Presidents lined the corridor; portraits of men who had led the nation through dangerous crises—yet none so dangerous as that which faced it now! Tension tightened the air in the famed dwelling. Operator 5's glance at his watch told him that he was keeping the urgent appointment to the minute.

A voice answered the rap of the Secret Service agent. "Come in!" Operator 5 strode into the impressive study, toward the grave faced man at the desk. The President rose, and his hand gripped Jimmy Christopher's. He said, solemnly:

"My boy, your name has been figuring prominently in advices sent me by General Staff—but I have not called you here in connection with that matter. There's a highly important mission to be performed. My faith in you makes me positive that you are the man to carry it out."

"Thank you, Mr. President."

Jimmy Christopher turned to the two men standing near the desk. One was Z-7—his face haggard, his eyes glowing with deep, dark flashes of light. The other was a huge man, with a dominating presence, a powerful, rugged face.

The President, gesturing toward him, said quietly: "Operator 5, this is Carter Case. You know, of course, that he is the greatest industrialist in the country. Mr. Case, I must ask you to keep Operator 5's identity a strict confidence. In the mission you are about to undertake together, he will be known as your secretary."

Carter Case's huge hand crushed upon Jimmy Christopher's. His was a name known around the world. Possessed of vast wealth, a personal friend of the rulers of nations, the leading exponent of the economic policy of mass production, a man of indomitable will and far-flung influence, he was an international figure.

Now, in throaty, heavy tones he said: "I consider it an honor to meet you, young man."

The President leaned forward intently. "Operator 5, Mr. Case had proposed a daring plan. He has verified my belief, first of all, that there is chiefly an economic reason for the Yellow invasion. He has volunteered to use his influence to turn this very motive back on the Yellow Command as one of our most powerful weapons."

"I will explain," Carter Case said briskly. "We are all aware, of course, that before this actual armed invasion occurred, the

INVASION OF THE YELLOW WARLORDS

United States was the target of a powerful economic war. The Yellow Empire, above all others, has been fighting us in the world market. Our industry has suffered from her attacks, and we in turn have tried to protect ourselves from her economic onslaughts."*

OPERATOR 5 nodded his understanding of this situation.

"She has been harassed in two ways," Carter Case continued.

---

* AUTHOR'S NOTE: Economic war against the United States has been waged for some time from the Orient. It is a well-known fact that Oriental laborers work for such low wages that American labor cannot possibly compete. Business in the United States has suffered, not only through the depreciation of the currencies of certain Pacific nations, but because raw material may be bought in the United States, freighted to these nations, manufactured into merchandise, returned to this country and can still be sold at prices beneath the cost of producing the same merchandise in the United States, at prevailing salary levels. As an instance, facts and figures were presented to the United States Tariff Commission last October to prove that due directly to Japanese competition, 36 American mills were forced to remain closed during the year, and between 7,500 and 10,000 workers normally employed in these mills were deprived of jobs. Walter Kamp, of the Delaware Rayon Company, declared that Japanese competition definitely killed the industry in this country. Similar effects have been felt in almost all industries within the United States. The toy industry in particular lies stricken by Japanese competitors who imitate American products and *sell* them here at prices half the cost of the *production price* in the United States.

Japan, to continue the parallel, was politically at peace with all nations as 1934 ended, but commercially at war with at least half the world. All the

"First, world powers have shut off her supplies of raw material, which has crippled her because she has no supplies within her own borders. Second, high tariffs have been erected against her so that she's lately been unable to sell what little merchandise she's been able to manufacture. With foreign sources of supply and foreign markets closed to her, the Yellow Empire has been forced to undertake armed aggression to reopen them."

"Her aim is, of course," Jimmy Christopher answered, "to confiscate our resources and to control our industry."

"Exactly. She is desperately trying to save herself from industrial and national doom—by annexing the United States! She intends to make of it a vast supply-base and market which she can control utterly. Her plan is, I think, plain. She intends to use the wealth of the United States to fight the economic forces of the entire world—to beat them down and dominate the globe industrially for all time."

"And the people within the United States—?" Operator 5 inquired.

"—Face horrible conditions. Our workers will be absolutely unable to compete with Yellow labor. They will either have to force themselves down to the intolerable existence level of the

large nations or their industrial groups began action early this year to restrict imports of Japanese manufactured goods.

During the year Japan was hit by trade restrictions in the British Empire, Italy, India, African areas and South America. The effect of these restrictions was to begin a serious crippling of Japanese export. The closing and restriction of foreign markets caused great concern within Japan.

Yellowese—work for a few cents a week and exist on that—or flee the country. Millions will be killed if the invasion assumes national proportions; the Yellowese will dominate the nation completely; our industry, our government, millions of Americans will be under complete Yellowese control."

"The invasion will cost you dearly, Mr. Case," Operator 5 declared.

"It will cost me a billion dollars worth of industrial holdings—but I am not thinking of that now," Carter Case answered. "I am thinking of the welfare of the nation, the people. I've proposed that I attempt a peace conference with the Yellow Counselor of Military Affairs, General Balta, who is commanding the Yellow expeditionaries here."

"You believe such a conference will stop the invasion?" Operator 5 asked. "That it will lead the Yellowese to withdraw?"

"It's a great gamble. It will be a proposal to create trade treaties between the United States and the Yellow Empire. It may remove their motive for the invasion. I am, you know, a personal friend of the Yellow Emperor. I have known Counselor Balta for many years. They will listen to me, I dare say, more sympathetically than to anyone else in this country. I want to use all my influence with them to induce them to withdraw under terms of concession."

"If they accept, it means that we have yielded—in a partial defeat!" Operator 5 exclaimed. "Trade treaties will mean terrific industrial competition—oppression that will force our people down to the wretched existence level of the Yellowese, in the end."

"It will save the lives of millions of our people," Carter Case pointed out. "It will preserve the United States as a nation, and keep it from becoming a colony of the Yellow Empire under armed rule. We are forced to admit that we face a great tragedy in this war, and a small tragedy is not too high a price to pay to save ourselves from it."

The President rose. "I have agreed that Mr. Case may use his influence with the Yellow Command. He will prepare the way for a treaty conference. If it is agreed, the exact terms cannot even be speculated upon now. It is a desperate gamble, but we believe the loss of billions of dollars of trade is better than the loss of millions of lives in a horrible war, even if we are victorious.

"The treaties will, of course, if they are signed, hold for only a number of years. During that time we'll be able to rebuild our national defenses. At the expiration date, we'll be able to renounce further treaties altogether, I hope. A period of terrific hardship may result, but in the end the United States will rise from it. Otherwise it may cease to exist altogether, in the most terrible war the world has ever known."

Operator 5 searched the grave eyes of the President, studied the face of Z-7, examined the powerful features of Carter Case. He asked quietly: "And my part?"

"Mr. Case proposed to fly into the war zone immediately the way is prepared for him. We will induce the Yellow Command to grant him a safe arrival and departure. You will accompany him as bodyguard, posing as his secretary. In effect you will become an unofficial representative of the government. We are aware that it is a highly dangerous mission, but—it is a gamble that must be played."

"Yes, sir."

"You are ready to accompany Mr. Case at a moment's notice?"

"I am, sir."

"Very well. I will inform you of—"

A knock interrupted the President. At his call, his Secretary strode into the zoom. In one hand he carried a dispatch, which he passed to the Chief Executive. He declared breathlessly:

"We've succeeded in communicating with General Balta in Los Angeles. He's agreed to the safe conduct of Mr. Case and one companion across the Yellow line and back. He will receive Mr. Case at the Yellow Field Headquarters!"

The President jerked up. "The way is prepared now! I'll order a plane for you at once. As soon as you're able to arrange for the trip—"

"We'll make the journey tonight, Mr. President," Carter Case declared. "Tonight—at the soonest moment possible!"

THE SWIFT Army plane roared through the glare of the floodlights at Bolling Field, across the smooth tarmac, into the chill night air, and drove into the west. Its destination lay far across the country, deep in the territory dominated by the Yellow invaders. It drove on its extraordinary mission through a night which spread blind terror across the nation.

Operator 5 sat at the controls. In the observation compartment, garbed in coveralls, hooded with a helmet, his powerful eyes covered with goggles, rode Carter Case.

Operator 5, as he plunged his plane away from the Capital, glanced down at the pattern of lights. Somewhere below, he knew, the trustworthy Tim Donovan was on watch—lurking in the dark, observing the building suspected of being the headquarters of dangerous espionage agents. Somewhere below General Staff was in session, their orders directing the Army westward, inexorably into the zone of war. Within that spiderweb of lights, the fate of a nation was entangled—perhaps with no hope that any man could extricate it.

Now cities streamed past, below them. In them, bulletin after bulletin circulated among the people, bringing heartening hope. News flashed that the Army was still moving west at fastest speed. The Atlantic Fleet was steaming into the Panamá Canal and would soon add its strength to the ships of the Pacific Squadron. The Yellow Line was still halted—no enemy advance was taking place.

Yet the entire Pacific coast was clamped under the merciless rule of the Yellowese. Great, menacing warships rode at anchor there, huge guns were trained at key cities, ready to flame out death in a new attack. Swarms of vessels of the Yellow merchant marine crowded to the docks of Long Beach, the Embarcadero of San Francisco, the piers of Seattle; and from them hordes of Yellow troops disembarked throughout all the western states the cancerous growth of the Yellow Empire was spreading.

All lines of communication had been seized. All means of transportation had been taken over by Yellow troops and were being used only for moving the invaders farther inland. Every police force had been disrupted. Thousands of United States enlisted men and officers, captured in the swift Yellow advance, were being held prisoners in police headquarters, schools, asylums, hotels, tenements. Every remaining unit of defense of the United States was now a weapon in the hands of the Yellowese.

Saffron-skinned troops patrolled the thoroughfares of every city and town. Americans, terrorized by the death which had stalked the streets, unable to defend themselves or to look for protection from our government, huddled in their flame-torn homes, ridden by diseases spread by polluted water, starving because all food supplies had been confiscated by the Yellow expeditionaries—completely dominated by the Yellow scourge.

Toward that stricken territory Operator 5 plunged his plane; and as his wings swept high across the white crested Rockies, dawn blended its many lights along the skyline.

AS THE brightening colors spread across the rugged terrain and Jimmy Christopher drove closer to his objective, he peered down and saw the main roads black with advancing, uniformed men. Great trucks were rumbling westward; field cannon were rolling; tanks were crawling like giant turtles; caissons were flocking; rank upon rank of U.S. Infantry were massing toward the Yellow line.

On open fields below, airplanes waited in readiness to fling themselves into the counter-attack when General Staff sounded the signal. From every Army post along the Mexican border, from every camp in the middle west and the northwest, from every air base east of the saffron bulwarks, the military strength of the nation was mobilizing for the conflict with an enemy on American soil. Beneath the wings of Operator 5's plane spread

Men retreated from the field pieces as terrific heat beat upon him!

a sight that was majestic and magnificent—and horrifying to one who realized that only disaster lurked ahead.

From a pocket of his tunic he withdrew a copy of the dispatch which had flashed to Washington over wires connecting with the camp of the enemy. It expressed consent to the mission of Carter Case, and stipulated a time and a wave-length for communicating with the Yellow Command during the approach of the plane. The moment was nearing now. Jimmy Christopher snapped the switch of the shortwave wireless apparatus and plugged the pins of his earphones into the jacks.

Immediately the tubes warmed, and a deafening splutter came out of the ether. The baffling disturbance roared violently at every setting of the dial, including the wave-band mentioned by the Yellow dispatch. The enemy forces were still "jamming" the air, making wireless communication impossible except for brief intervals when the ether was cleared for their own use. Now, unbrokenly, the crackling continued, cutting off the flying plane's only means of communication.

Operator 5 silenced the roar with a click of the switch and peered overside. He was nearing, he knew, the dread Yellow line which stretched across United States soil. Below, on the roads and in the fields, the military units of the U.S. Army were spreading, building a front against the Yellow hordes. Field headquarters were being established, cannon taking position, kitchens being set up, field hospitals tented—an army settling down for the business of battle. And he saw—

The signs of the mysterious heat-force!

A strange suspension of movement hushed the occupied area

below. Men became motionless in wonder. Giant trucks crawled to a stop on the roads. Cannon crews poised in amazement, as into the air came a strange heat which rapidly became stifling. Swiftly, throughout the vast spread of the military below, the invisible force of the enemy played.

Soaring high overhead, Operator 5 felt none of the destructive heat—but he saw men dropping tools and guns that were suddenly too hot to hold. He saw scores and hundreds begin to swarm across the fields in a frantic endeavor to escape a suffocation they could not escape. He saw men retreat from the field guns as blistering radiations beat from the iron. Quickly, bringing binoculars to his eyes, he examined the phenomenon as a scientist watches the behavior of microscopic creatures beneath his lenses—and as he watched, the first glow came.

GUNS AND tools thrown to the ground began to shine—growing red, becoming white. The cannon gave off a dull radiance that brightened quickly. Trucks chuffed to a stop, their chassis softening under their loads. Flame burst from them as sizzling metal brought fire to tarpaulins and wood. Loaded guns exploded while no fingers touched the white hot triggers. Terrific blasts of flame and fumes tore the earth as magazines of high-explosives roared up. Giant trucks vanished in the bursts of cataclysmic power.

In a nearby field airplanes, abandoned by their terrorized pilots, sank on melted tires—and blew to fragments as their fuel tanks unleashed tearing power. Flying, white hot fragments of torn metal rained like enemy shrapnel, mowing down men by scores. Within a few moments the fields below became a no-man's-land where life could not exist.

Officers, running crazily with their men, ripped buttons from their uniforms—buttons that shone white hot—with hands that sizzled to the bone at the touch. They flung off any metal on their uniforms. They swarmed, seeing the field cannon shining hotly, trucks disintegrating into molten masses of flaming metal, caissons dropping apart, while hundreds around them shrieked in terror and strove to escape the inescapable doom.

The penetrating power was coagulating the very brains of those it played upon, turning them into maniacs! A sane, level headed man of science ran muttering from his tent, across a field torn by destruction, into a screaming mob of madmen!

From the sky Operator 5 watched the horror of the mounting force. Within a few moments the awful power mounted to the height of its destructiveness. At the first indication of it, his hand had again darted to the switch of the short-wave installation. Now, as the deafening buzzing sounded through the phones, he trimmed his oscillator and called sharply into the spidered microphone.

"Calling GS! Operator 5 calling General Staff, Washington!"

The baffling disturbance of the ether still rang in Jimmy Christopher's ears; and he knew that his voice could not penetrate it. In desperation he shouted; even as he realized that nothing could carry his words to the War Department building.

"Calling GS! GS! For God's sake, order the military to retreat! The advance units are being destroyed! Order retreat! GS! GS!"

But no single syllable of Jimmy Christopher's voice could

reach through that strife-torn sky to General Staff. The warning vanished in utter ethereal turmoil.

CHAPTER 6
TRAITOR'S BRAND

B ELOW THE wings of Operator 5's speeding plane the scene changed now to one of ominous tranquility. Behind him he left the destruction-torn area across which the invisible power had played. Beneath him now lay territory as heavily protected by armed forces—the advance line of the Yellow invaders.

Deep trenches stretched as far as he could see. Roads were barricaded. Camps had been set up, and Yellow troops were strung along the line. Gun batteries glittered in the rising sun. Gleaming banks of anti-aircraft concentrations pointed their menacing snouts upward—though they did not bark as the lone American plane droned overhead: word had been flashed from the Yellow Command that the craft must pass unharmed.

Grimly Operator 5 watched the electric clock on the dash. He had kept the wireless switch turned on; now he trimmed it to the designated wave-length. The weariness of the long hours of his flight vanished and his nerves freshened as the appointed time neared.

And suddenly the static ceased. Quiet pervaded the ether. Out of it a high pitched voice spoke clipped syllables which rang clearly in Jimmy Christopher's phones.

"Honorable Carter Case, with compliments of Yellow

Command, is requested to descend upon field formerly called Glendale Airport, now known as Fuchu."

The instant the voice stopped, the loud sputtering returned. Jimmy Christopher nudged his controls, swinging the nose of the plane toward the field outside embattled Los Angeles.

As he approached, he peered down at a spread of destruction which appalled him. Vast areas of homes had been razed by fire; the tall City Hall was a toppled wreck; the business section of the city was a shambles. Shells and bombs, opening the way for the invaders, had made the white City of Angels into a soot-blackened City of Yellow Devils.

His blood ran cold as he swung the pursuit down to the airport. The tarmac bore the scars of planes that had exploded under the invisible Yellow power; but the damage had been repaired. Slant-eyed troops patrolled the road leading to it; other guarded its boundaries; Yellow battle planes sat on the smooth sand. It was into a center of enemy military operations, that Operator 5 directed his ship.

Yellow troops swarmed upon it, after its three-point landing. Peering into the expressionless saffron faces, he realized that if these Orientals chose, he and Carter Case would die on the spot.

The Yellowese formed a circle, shoulder to shoulder, around the plane and held their weapons ready. But once in position, they made no further move, and Jimmy Christopher climbed wearily from the pit, Carter Case at his side.

SUDDENLY THE circle parted. A Yellow lieutenant strode smartly into the cleared area. His uniform fitted his small body like a glove; his movements were precise as the functioning of

88

machinery; his saffron face was inscrutable, his black eyes a glittering puzzle.

He bowed, and spoke in a high voice, his words clipped by tight lips.

"To Honorable Carter Case, esteemed citizen of United States, friend of Heavenly Majesty the Emperor—your servant, General Balta, Counselor of Military Affairs of Yellow Empire, humbly offers felicitations and greetings."

Carter Case spoke calmly. "Please convey to the great General Balta my plea that it is I who am honored by his gracious consent to receive me, and beg him to accept the good wishes of his humble friend."

The lieutenant bowed. "If American gentleman will be so kind as to follow me, I will conduct you to headquarters of General Balta at once."

Operator 5 smiled tightly at the effusive and empty exchange of courtesies. He strode beside the huge Carter Case and the lieutenant, across the field. A Yellow squad smartly followed, then about-faced to guard the entrance when they stepped into the office building, which had once housed the executives of a great commercial airport. Inside the office stood several straight backed Yellow officers; these the lieutenant briskly faced.

"It is unworthy wish of General Balta that he see esteemed friend alone," said one.

Case and Operator 5 exchanged swift glances. Jimmy Christopher nodded. "I'll wait here," he said.

The lieutenant turned smartly again, opened a door. Carter Case strode through it. Before it closed, Operator 5 glimpsed the man who advanced to meet him, smiling, hand outstretched. General Balta, Counselor of Military Affairs of the Yellow Empire, directing power of the enemy invasion. The huge American's hand gripped the small one of the slant-eyed, saffron faced military genius—and the door closed.

Operator 5 waited at attention, feeling the eyes of the Yellow officers fixed inscrutably upon him, hearing the rumbling voice of Carter Case mingle with the high pitched tones of General Balta, in words which were to decide the path of history.

At that precise moment, though he did not know it—in the great building of the Department of War in Washington, D.C., Major-General Falk, in conference with the other members of the Joint Board, was peering appalled at a dispatch which informed them of the devastating attack by the invisible Yellow power upon the advancing Army.

Guns destroyed! Ammunition lost! Men turned into maniacs! Our advance disrupted!

The Yellow Command had struck its first blow at them on land. And there was only one possible answer to that; an even more concerted advance of their own military!

"We'll fight along that Yellow line until we break it and drive those devils back into the sea!" the Chief of Staff was thundering.

While, in the little room far across the country, the voices of Carter Case and General Balta sounded in turn and in the outer office Operator 5 waited.

IN HIS study in the White House, the President of the United States sat at his desk, alert to each communication brought him in quick succession by his secretaries. One brought the light of hope into his eyes:

"The Atlantic Fleet has passed through the Panamá Canal and is now proceeding under full steam to join the Pacific Squadron."

One brought despair: "Devastating attack on our Army by invisible force exerted by Yellowese has seriously crippled our military forces and is undermining the morale of our men whom the Power did not touch."

One brought uncertainty: "Trans-Atlantic passenger liners following usual sea lanes have reported sighting many ships, nationality unknown, toward the south. These ships are proceeding under minimum speed, or have hoved to. Officer of *Ultima* reports his opinion that these are ships of the Yellowese merchant marine. If this is true, it means that the Yellow Command is preparing to strike again from the east!"

Into the streets of New York and the other great cities of the nation, newspapers poured, while the air remained blanketed by the constant interference broadcast by the Yellowese. Millions read startling headlines, their terror increased by the uncertainty which made it impossible for anyone to sift fact from rumor:

YELLOW ARMAMENT SUPPLY FROM EUROPE!
YELLOW SUB SIGHTED OFF CAPE HATTERAS!
WESTWARD MOVEMENT OF ARMY LEAVES
EAST UNDER-PROTECTED!

Fear mounted in the hearts of millions while, far in the west, in the armed camp of the enemy, a civilian backed by millions in wealth, and an enemy general backed by millions of armed men, spoke of the price of peace.

In the secret offices of WDC-13, headquarters of the United States Intelligence Service, the man known only as Z-7 sat tensely at his desk as dispatchers carried terse messages to him from the communications room.

"Can't raise SF, sir. Our San Francisco headquarters no longer exists."

"No answer from SW, chief. The Seattle office has apparently been seized by the Yellowese."

"All teletype wires to the West Coast are dead. Our telephone lines have been cut. We are absolutely isolated from every Intelligence operator in the invaded area."

Z-7's fist rapped the desk. "Blind! Struck blind! Our men in that area are helpless! We have no hope of sending other agents among those damned Yellowese!"

A dispatcher wagged his head. "If only Operator 5 had carried out your orders, we could already be rebuilding our organization and—"

"Don't speak of that!" Z-7 snapped. "Don't remind me of it! God! The charges that might be pressed against Operator 5 now—"

He broke off, staring at a fresh communication brought from the wireless table.

WDC-13—SPECIAL REPORT—RECONNAIS-
SANCE PLANE REPORTS YELLOW SQUAD-
RON STEAMING SOUTHWARD ALONG PACIFIC

COAST TOWARD PANAMA CANAL—WALTON, COMMANDING, "OKLAHOMA."

THE YOUNG man who, as temporary Commander of the Pacific Fleet, had ordered its withdrawal from the battle area, at that very moment stood at attention, his nerves tight, while the conference between Carter Case and General Balta came to an end.

Out through the connecting door the great industrial magnate had strode, and now General Balta bowed and, smiling benignly, his poise that of an animated yet graven image, closed it behind him.

Furrows darkened Case's forehead, his eyes glittered as he said to Operator 5: "We return to Washington at once!"

"May I ask, sir—?"

"I've failed! With the utmost politeness, General Balta held his ground. He told me very suavely that the Yellowese Command will continue its advance until the entire United States surrenders to the Yellow Emperor! He is completely confident of victory!"

The lieutenant who had escorted them before now stepped forward smartly.

"We are grieved that honor of visit must pass so soon, esteemed sir."

Jimmy Christopher strode beside Carter Case across the field. He sensed a marked alertness on the part of the officers who marched after them. He noted a Yellow battle plane drawn alongside his own Army pursuit plane, its prop whipping over.

The lieutenant suddenly turned and bowed to Case. "Lest

93

unfortunate accident befall you, esteemed sir," he remarked, "allow us great privilege of placing one of our own airplanes at your disposal. It will carry you across line far more safely than American ship. I beg to be allowed to place at disposal our most skilled pilot, Lieutenant Orke."

The smartly uniformed officer standing beside the Yellow plane bowed and came to attention.

"Your secretary, esteemed sir, may take American plane back. It has been refueled. I regret that we cannot offer him similar protection. Please honor us, esteemed sir, with your consent. We ask only that Lieutenant Orke be allowed safe conduct back to field."

Case gestured impatiently. "Yes, yes!"

He growled at Operator 5: "These gestures must be accepted. If you have no objection—"

"As you please, Mr. Case."

Jimmy Christopher stood back alertly while the great industrial magnate climbed into the pit of the Yellow plane. He noted that slant-eyed soldiers remained station around his own while Lieutenant Orke took the controls of the other. The slashing prop rolled the Yellow ship onto the runway; Case signaled a farewell to Jimmy Christopher. The Yellow plane crossed the smooth sand and lifted into the air.

Operator 5 turned to his own crate as the enemy plane soared high, streaking east swiftly. He climbed in and settled to the controls, feeling an uncanny warning of danger play coldly along his spine, and looked into the inscrutable faces of the officers confronting him. The lieutenant stepped forward, his expression unchanging, and again spoke in his emotionless, clipped tones.

"Lest we seem unappreciative of graciousness of visit, I beg to inform you that we count ourselves highly honored, and we implore you to believe that we hope for equally safe journey into east for you also—Operator 5."

Jimmy Christopher's darkened eyes flashed from face to face. His hand darted swiftly to the butt of his automatic nestled inside his coveralls. But none of the officers near the plane was making a movement. Their eyes, their faces, were still masked by the same unreadable expressionlessness. Then, almost imperceptibly, a ghost of a smile played along the lips of the lieutenant.

"As our cousins, Japanese, say, Operator 5—*banzai!*"

"Which means," Operator 5 translated quietly, " 'may you live a thousand years!' "

He sensed the sly irony of the word as he freed the brakes. His eyes kept alert as he opened the throttle. None of the officers so much as moved a finger as he sent the plane rolling across the sand.

It swooped before a howling backwash, gathering speed, its tail lifting. Then it sliced into the air and Jimmy Christopher drove it into the east under full power. He glanced back as he climbed, and saw the men on the field still standing motionless as statues.

THE MOCKING word echoed in his ears. *Banzai!* Uttered with wry contempt, it did not signify a wish that Operator 5 might live a thousand years. It expressed, he knew, the hope that he might die a thousand deaths—and yet the cunning Yellow devils were allowing him to fly safely from the field, to begin a swift trip toward the east and safety.

Why? The question was tantalizing. He half expected an onslaught of antiaircraft guns as he passed above the field—but it did not come. The officers were actually allowing him to put mile after mile behind him, to roar swiftly toward the Yellow line. Was it there that they intended to trap him?

He peered ahead. The plane carrying Carter Case had vanished by now. He gazed overside, and discerned in the distance the enemy camp which marked the farthest advance of the saffron flood. He climbed higher, waiting for the first crack of the anti-aircraft batteries; but the guns did not cough, no shells streaked up into the zenith. Below the wings of his plane, slowly, the Yellow line passed and receded.

Why?

Suddenly the answer came. The air flowing past his head and shoulders became quickly warm. An oppressive feverishness spread over his body. All the metal around him was beginning to heat, to radiate the strange invisible power that had become the most devastating weapon of war in the world. With a moan of despair he sent the pursuit plunging ahead at top speed, knowing that the unseeable doom was playing upon him. But he did not escape it.

The warmth became suffocating heat. Quickly he reached beneath the seat of the pit, into the space provided for the parachute pack. He had, with customary caution, checked that vital piece of equipment before leaving Bolling Field. In Washington the parachute had rested in its place. Now he groped into—emptiness! The Yellowese had removed his parachute.

The penetrating heat could not wipe away the icy chill that gathered around his heart at that moment. He straightened in the pit, shaking off his coveralls, ripping off his goggles, tearing the helmet from his head. Every particle of metal on the plane was radiating heat of a scorching intensity. The power was playing as well upon the metal fuel tanks, heating them to a point at which an explosion would be inevitable.

Swiftly he unclicked his safety belt and stood up, against the tearing wind. He let the plane mush into a glide as he struggled into the rear cubby. Inadvertently his hands touched metal that was glowing red. He groped quickly in the space in the observation pit where another parachute should have been stored—and again found nothing. Both chutes had been stolen from the plane! And it was becoming a comet in the sky, a thing shining from boss to tail with a sizzling warning of destruction!

DESPERATELY OPERATOR 5 clambered back to the controls. He threw the stick forward and sent the crate plunging downward at full throttle. But swift as the dive was, the devastating force kept enveloping it. Strive as he might, he could not escape it.

The fever in his body became an unbearable torture. He felt a numbness creeping through his mind—and remembered maddened men running on a flame-torn field. Blistering heat played upon him as he drove the plane down, while a field expanded like a stretched rubber sheet before his eyes.

The pain became almost unendurable as he swooped lower

and lower. He brought the blistering tires toward an earth which blurred before his eyes. He saw the wings fuming, felt a bubbling jolting of the boiling fuel tanks. He pressed the brakes, and white hot drums caused the bands to burst into flames—the brakes would not hold. With the motor cut, with the propeller a slashing white thing twisting out of shape, he scrambled desperately over the cowling and flung himself headlong.

He struck the ground, rolled, and lay face up with his clothing smouldering—and the last flicker of consciousness dimmed in his mind. He did not see the plane hurtling crazily across the field. He did not hear its terrific concussion. He lay unconscious while fragments of the sundered plane rained from the churning, smoke-blackened air and while rumbling echoes rolled back from the mountains.

CHAPTER 7
TREASON BY AIR

SECRET WALLS shielded the existence of central headquarters WDC-13 of the United States Intelligence Service. The windowless rooms, accessible only through secret doors, to only a few of the most trusted undercover agents of the government, were crowded with file cabinets, teletype and radio receivers which kept incessantly busy. WDC-13 was the center of the invisible spider-web of secrecy which functioned for the preservation of the nation—a web the western strands of which had now been ripped down by Yellow hands.

Z-7, chief of the undercover forces of the Intelligence, paced anxiously back and forth across his hidden office. He strode to his desk as dispatchers hurried to it with fresh communications from the western front. His dark eyes smoldered as advice after advice filled out the pattern of chaotic destruction that was striking across the country.

WDC-13—YELLOW SQUADRON STILL STEAM-ING TOWARD PANAMA CANAL—WALTON, COMMANDING, "OKLAHOMA."

Another:

YELLOW FORCES SWARMING FROM MANDATE ISLANDS—U.S. NAVAL BASE AT GUAM COMPLETELY SURROUNDED—SEIZURE OF PHIL-IPPINES A CERTAINTY—DEFENSE IMPOSSIBLE—MPI.*

ADVANCING U.S. MILITARY ROUTED AGAIN

* AUTHOR'S NOTE: The Mandate Islands of the Yellow Empire, in the Pacific, created a dangerous international situation months before the Yellow inva-sion of the United States occurred. These islands, tiny dots in the Pacific, are of vital strategic importance since they constitute stepping-stones to the Philippines, and completely surrounded Guam, where a highly import-ant base of the U.S. Navy is located. The islands are about 1,400 in number, contain about 800 square miles and a population of some 50,000.

The United States has demanded international supervision of these islands, in accordance with established mandate treaties covering them, and this the Yellow Empire has strenuously resisted. Great Britain, France and Italy consider that these islands are not the property of the Yellow government,

BY ATTACKS OF INVISIBLE POWER. HUNDREDS
KILLED IN EXPLOSIONS, HUNDREDS DRIVEN MAD
BY EFFECT OF HEAT—GENERAL STAFF MAIN-
TAINING ADVANCE.

Z-7 snatched at the telephone as the bell chattered. The voice
that came over the line was quick, breathless—Tim Donovan's.

while the Yellow Empire considers that they are, and will tolerate no interference.

Months before the Yellow invasion of the United States, the Empire began
to fortify the islands, which resulted in protest from other world powers.
Harbors were reconstructed, new piers built, new anchorages provided. A
resolution demanding an investigation by the Senate Foreign Relations
Committee into recurrent reports that the Yellow Empire was fortifying
the islands was introduced into the United States Senate. The resolution set
forth that if the Yellow Empire was doing so, she was acting in violation of
the Treaty of Versailles and also in violation of the mandate terms.

A renowned student of international affairs recently stated on the subject:
"A study of the Yellow Empire's attitude toward the mandated islands in
the Pacific discloses that the Empire is determined to defy the rest of the
world in maintaining possession of these highly valuable strategic points.
The Empire has, in effect, told the League of Nations and the world that
if anyone wants to take these islands away from her, they will have to do it
by force."

The above dispatch, to which this note refers, discloses that the Yellow
Empire has made full use of her mandate islands as points of attack upon
outlying American possessions at a time when American defense of them
is impossible.

"Chief! Isn't there any word from Jimmy?"

"None," Z-7 answered. "Absolutely none! Carter Case made a safe return to Bolling Field, but Operator 5 is still missing. No reports concerning him have been received. We can only wait—wait!"

"Gee, Chief!" Tim pleaded. "Jimmy'll come back, won't he? He's got to come back!"

"Keep in touch with me, Tim," Z-7 directed in a husky tone. "Call me again—and we'll hope that next time there'll be word from Operator 5."

AS Z-7 replaced the telephone it shrilled again. This time a heavier, officious voice came over the wire. The Washington chief recognized it as that of the Secretary of War.

"Please come to my office at once, Z-7. There is a matter of the utmost importance to be considered. The entire fate of our western expedition may depend on it."

Z-7 strode from his desk, snapping over his shoulder to the chief dispatcher who came to the connecting door: "Call me at the War Department if there's word from Operator 5!" Anxiously, through a hidden elevator, past secret doors, he sought his way to the street and a waiting car.

After a few moments of swift driving, he entered the building of the War Department and was conducted at once to the office of the Secretary. There he discovered Major-General Falk, Chief of Staff, and Brigadier-General Hartwell, War Plans Division. He sensed the tension of a new crisis in the air.

The Secretary of War, gripping the Washington chief's hand hotly, spoke in tight syllables.

"Operator 5, you are under arrest!" Jimmy Christopher stood
unmoving. "This station will be destroyed tonight!"

"You, as well as we, Z-7, are coping with a tremendous task.
You are striving to discover the headquarters of the sabotage
agents who are preying upon our mobilized war material manu-
facturers. We are working under a terrific handicap in order to
make the supplies our forces need, and these damnable sabotage

agents are making the problem a hundred times more difficult. You are doing your utmost—but now, at this moment, an even greater emergency faces us."

"You are assured of my complete cooperation, gentlemen," Z-7 declared.

"That emergency has to do with the complete demoralization of our advancing Army!" the Secretary of War asserted. "The attacks by the Yellow invisible power are devastating enough, but now there is a new force which has become even more destructive. Spoken words—a broadcast incitement to widespread mutiny!"

The Secretary turned quickly to a console radio. A moment after he clicked the switch, an ear-rending clatter issued from it—the everlasting disturbance thrown into the ether by the Yellow forces in order to make all broadcasting impossible. Allowing the sputter to continue, the Secretary snapped at Z-7:

"At intervals that noise ceases, when the Yellow Command needs to use the air. During those intervals, a powerful broadcasting station seizes the opportunity to spread sedition. A man speaking in English—an American, it's certain—preaches revolt among our Army. In spite of all our efforts, his words reach our men and officers in the west—and by God, sir, unless it's stopped, it will mean the mutiny of our entire military force— mean our being struck helpless before the advance of the Yellow invaders!"

Z-7 began: "You have not informed me—"

"Because your staff is already overloaded with work—because we tried to discover the location of that station by means of our naval radio-direction finders. We have utterly failed. Now the locating and destruction of that radio station has become of the utmost importance. You must throw every available man into the field in order to—"

THE SECRETARY broke off as the sputter from the radio abruptly ceased. The air became serenely clear. On a wavelength far beyond the broadcast band, the Yellow Command was at that moment sending a coded wireless message. But the next moment, loudly and resonantly, a voice began to speak.

"Men of the United States Army! Refuse to be led into utter destruction! Turn your forces back east! Rebel against being ordered to slaughter yourselves in a horribly unequal battle! Revolt against your officers! Save yourselves and our Army by retreat!"

Z-7's face paled as he listened. The voice went on.

"Citizens of the west! Cooperate to save our Army from complete rout! Refuse food to our troops unless they are retreating eastward! Refuse to billet them! Deny them every necessity until they revolt against their murderous orders! Turn the Army back!"

The Washington chief froze with dismay as the officers of the General Staff and the Secretary stared at him.

"Men of the Navy! Mutiny alone can save you and our ships from plunging to the bottom of the sea! Make prisoners of your officers who refuse to stay out of range of the Yellow naval squadrons! Do not attempt to stop the Yellow battleships from entering the Panamá Canal! Save yourselves and your ships for the moment when we can strike without facing absolutely certain annihilation!"

As the last words sounded, the deafening crackle again came into the air. It drowned out the voice. The Secretary clicked the switch of the radio, and silence came into the room. His knuckles rapped as he declared:

"That voice *is* arousing mutiny in our military and naval forces! Already there have been uprisings, mass refusals to follow orders! Our war plans are disrupted by it! It is making victory by the Yellow invaders a certainty! Z-7, you must find that station! You must silence that voice!" Z-7's throat was tight and dry. With great difficulty, his tones husky and strained, he declared: "I am forced to agree with you, gentlemen. That station must be destroyed. That speaker must pay the full penalty for his act. I—I know who he is. I recognized his voice."

"What! You know—?"

"Operator 5."

Major-General Falk stared. "Operator 5, then," he thundered, "has turned traitor to the United States!"

The Secretary of War snapped: "He must be found and taken prisoner! He must pay the full penalty for treason!"

Z-7's eyes were dimmed with agony. "Gentlemen," he said raspingly, "I know where that station is located. Let us waste no time with explanations now. Operator 5 must be taken into custody at once. If you will—follow me—"

The Washington chief broke off as words failed him, and turned stiffly to the door.

A STEADY crackle as of violent static echoed through the board-walled room from the small receiving set. Mingled with the sound was the muffled drone of dynamos whirring beyond a closed door. Before the little receiver, alert for the first instant when the sputtering would again cease, ready to speak again into the microphone that hurled his words to the four corners of the nation and beyond, stood Operator 5.

His cheeks were sunken, his eyes haggard. His shoulders

sagged with fatigue. But his eyes gleamed with indomitable purpose.

He stood alone in a room beneath the surface of the earth. Black panels walled it, studded with meters and switches. A bare globe shone overhead. Adjoining the room were others, housing the power supply of the hidden radio station. The secret cavity could be reached only through a narrow cleft of rock hidden in a wood which lay far outside Washington. Bit by bit, part by part, when an earlier national crisis had demanded it, this equipment had been brought to the underground chambers and secretly erected.*

The grave emergency in which this powerful station had first been used was past; it had remained unused since the success of the strategy for which Operator 5 had designed it; and now he had sought his way back to it alone, driven by a conviction he could not shake, obsessed with a purpose he must serve.

A long, exhausting trek had brought him here. By any means he could find, after he had recovered consciousness on the field to which he had driven the doomed plane, he had sought his way back east, by wagon, by car, begging rides, stealing lifts—until

---

* AUTHOR's NOTE: This secret broadcasting station, equipped to radiate "swirl-waves" which defy the most accurate direction-finders, constructed under the personal direction of Roger Wentling Morlin, the eminent physicist working under the War Department, became a vital part of a nation-wide attack led by Operator 5 against the despotism of President Ursus Young. The full details are included in the amazing adventure of Operator 5 called "Blood Reign of the Dictator."

at last he had reached an airport. Taking not even a moment to report to WDC-13, he had achieved his destination—this secret radio station.

At every mile of his agonized return trip he had heard appalling news of American losses along the Yellow line—of the devastating destruction wrought by the invisible Yellow power. Each added report had strengthened his determination. Each reported blow of the heat-force had strengthened his determination to make use of the only possible way he could combat the annihilating orders of General Staff—this secret radio station.

Hunger weakened him, thirst burned his throat, exhaustion throbbed through his body as he listened to the continued "jamming" of the air and waited for the interval of quiet into which he might again thrust his plea.

Suddenly the crackling stopped. The little radio set hummed quietly. Immediately he pressed the blades of a huge knife-switch home and brought the microphone close to his lips.

"Men of the Army and Navy! Look before you and see certain, utter destruction! See inevitable death! See the complete helplessness of our nation once all defenses are destroyed! Know that the orders of General Staff are forcing you to the brink of death! Know that General Staff is unwittingly inviting the triumph of the Yellow forces over the entire nation! You have higher orders than theirs, men of the Army and Navy! You owe a greater allegiance to your nation! Preserve it by revolt—until the moment comes when we may marshal our forces into a victorious drive!"

Again the sputter broke into the last words. Jimmy Christopher unknifed the switch, clicked off the microphone, silenced the little receiving set. He turned away slowly, despair lining his face, hopelessness dimming his eyes. He left the room wearily, crossing another huge cavity where a rotary printing press sat— another weapon which he had once used to perpetuate the nation, but which was useless now. He strode past, to the last door, his intention being to leave the hidden rooms under cover of dark.

He stopped short, as the latch of the great door clicked. His hand flicked to his armpit holster—as the door swung open swiftly. Immediately he dropped his hand, and squared his shoulders. At stiff attention he faced the men who had entered.

Z-7. Major-General Falk. Brigadier-General Hartwell. The Secretary of War. Four brother operators of the United States Intelligence. Four who leveled automatics at him.

"You are under arrest!"

The Chief of Staff snapped it. Silence followed the clicking words. Jimmy Christopher stood unmoving. Two of his fellow undercover agents stepped beside him and relieved him of his automatic. He peered unflinchingly at Z-7.

"This station will be destroyed tonight, my boy," the Washington chief declared gravely. "It will never be used again. I have no alternative but to take you into custody."

"I understand, Chief."

Two of the men strode past Jimmy Christopher. General Hartwell trod after them. His shoulders sagged again when he heard the cracking shots, the crashing sounds, which meant that the great amplifying tubes of the station were being broken. He heard other shots as bullets ripped into the vital coils and condensers of the equipment. Then, stiffly, the Chief of Staff turned away, and Z-7 gestured.

Operator 5 followed his chief along a bare-walled tunnel, through a narrow cleft of rock, out into the chill night—a prisoner of war.

OPERATOR 5 stood at rigid attention, facing Z-7 across the desk, in the inner office of WDC-13. General Falk sat beside the Washington chief, his eyes icy. From an adjoining room came the clatter of teletypes as fresh reports streamed into the headquarters. These were forgotten now. A member of the Intelligence service, accused of high crimes in time of war, stood before his chief.

"You understand, my boy," Z-7 said huskily, "our procedure in a matter of this kind. Fortunately for us, an offense like yours occurs only rarely in the service. I am grieved, more than I can tell you, that my duty requires me to press the charges against you, for you are as dear to me as a son. You will be tried before a tribunal of your fellow officers. They will consider the evidence. They will decide your guilt and pronounce sentence upon you. Before you are brought before them, you have an opportunity to explain—now."

"I have no defense, Chief," Operator 5 declared. "I admit my guilt."

Z-7 winced. "You face serious consequences, my boy. Why—in God's name, why did you do it?"

Operator 5's eyes darkened. "I warned General Staff that I would do everything in my power to counteract their orders. I am ever more convinced now than I was that our Army is certain to be destroyed if their strategy continues. It is an absolutely fatal move! If I am guilty of treason, it is because I am pledged to maintain—not the stupidities of General Staff, but the welfare of the nation!"

Major-General Falk's face went white with fury. Z-7 rose slowly, his face a graven mask. Jimmy Christopher leaned forward; and now his words carried the ring of steel.

"We have no defense against the heat-force of the enemy. Our western advance is giving the enemy a chance to turn it upon us and spread utter devastation. You have already seen the first results. If the Army persists in advancing, it will be completely destroyed. If our Navy attempts to stop the advance of the Yellow fleet toward the Panamá Canal, it will be plunged to the bottom of the ocean. On land and on sea and in the air we will be left utterly defenseless—because General Staff has blindly ordered it!

"Once our Army is crushed, the Yellowese will swarm east. Once our Navy is sunk the east will be without protection and a second invasion will sweep in from the Atlantic. Invasion from the west! Attack from the east! Our nation, our people caught in the jaws of a war trap! No possible hope of rescue! Then the United States will cease to exist and this nation will become a colony of the Yellow Empire!"

General Falk sneered. Z-7's eyes flickered with uncertainty as he listened. Jimmy Christopher pressed on.

"That's the plan of the Yellow command, plain to be seen. Our only possible hope from that fate is to preserve our defenses against the time when we can fight the Yellow forces on equal terms. Let's learn the secret of their heat-force and turn it back on them. Let's back it up with an Army and Navy saved from annihilation by retreat! Then we'll be certain of victory—a victory which is utterly impossible now!"

OPERATOR 5'S knuckles rapped the desk sharply. "That's why I fought General Staff single-handed. The penalties I'll suffer for my act are nothing to be compared with the certain, utter defeat of the United States in this war. If I had the choice to make again, I would follow the same course with all my heart and soul. My only regret is that I will not, as a prisoner of war, be able to keep on fighting the officers and the orders which are bringing certain doom to my country."

Major-General Falk rose and stood rigid. "I have heard you through, Operator 5. Nothing you've said has convinced me that our military strategy must be altered. We'll persist in our plan. The fact remains that General Staff holds you responsible for the success of the Yellow invasion in the west. You've committed serious crimes against your government. General Staff is not yet ready to accept the military advice of a—traitor."

Jimmy Christopher winced as the word rang in his ears. His dark gaze shifted to the haggard face of Z-7. The Washington chief spoke huskily.

"It is my duty, my boy, greatly as I regret it, to hold you prisoner. It will be my duty to execute a sentence upon you once it is decided upon by a court of your fellow agents. You'll be obliged to face trial for inciting to mutiny, and full punishment will be exacted from you. There is—nothing more I can say."

The telephone shrilled. It rang a second time, and the Washington chief touched a button on his desk, in response to which the door of the inner office opened. The two brother operators who had seized Jimmy Christopher in the underground rooms now advanced to his side. Z-7 ordered them raspingly:

"Take the prisoner away."

Strong hands closed on his arms as the telephone clattered a third time. Automatically Z-7 lifted the instrument. An eager voice rang over the line, and Z-7 answered it with an agonized "Yes—yes, I have heard—he is here." He looked up, as Jimmy Christopher was about to step through the door, and said quietly:

"Tim Donovan is on the line, my boy.

Perhaps—your last chance to speak with him—you'd better—"

Operator 5 turned back wretchedly, as words failed Z-7. He pressed the receiver to his ear, and his face grew dark with pain as the eager tones of the tough little Irish lad reached him.

"Jimmy! Gee, I'm glad you're back! Gosh, I thought something awful'd happened to you, Jimmy!"

Operator 5 forced himself to say: "I'm okay, old timer. All okay."

"Jimmy, listen!" The boy's voice quickened. "I haven't been off the job of watching that house since you put me on it! Night and day, Jimmy! I stuck because you told me to, until I heard from you! Nothing happened—nothing at all—until just now!"

Operator 5 snapped to alertness. "What is it, Tim? What have you seen?"

"A man went into the house a few minutes ago! I saw his face! It was the espionage agent who tampered with your boat!

Right after him came two more men and a woman. They're in there now. They must've been laying low, playing safe, but now they're using that place again. Gee, Jimmy, it's a red-hot lead—we've got to follow it!"

TORTURE SURGED through Operator 5. He whispered, "Hold the line, Tim!" and peered at Z-7. "Chief," he said quietly, "will you allow me a few hours of freedom? Long enough to follow a new lead that—"

"It's impossible!"

Jimmy Christopher's eyes gleamed. "Then, Chief, listen to me! Tim has unearthed a new lead that—"

"Under the circumstances, Operator 5," Z-7 cut in sharply, "I am bound to disregard totally any information you might give me. Coming as it does from a prisoner of war, from a man who had confessed himself guilty of—treason—"

The chief broke off, again finding the difficulty of the words too much for him; but the smouldering blackness of his eyes was alive with unflinchable determination. Jimmy Christopher stood motionless, and despair came into his heart.

"Chief, you won't listen to—?"

"I can't, my boy! I can't!"

Suddenly, grimly, Operator 5 raised the telephone to his lips.

"Tim! Orders! Keep on the job—and wait!"

"Count on me, Jimmy!"

Operator 5 lowered the instrument. He turned quickly to the door, and again the hands of his two brother undercover agents fastened upon his arms. He stepped into the corridor, paused, and gazed back at Z-7.

114

"It's okay, Chief," he said quietly. "You're doing the only thing possible. Good luck and—so long."

There was a sharp edge in his voice which still rasped the smarting nerves of Z-7 after the door closed....

Jimmy Christopher advanced between the two operators to a panel in the corridor wall. One of them touched a button; in response machinery whirred. Presently the panel slid aside automatically, disclosing the cab of the secret elevator. He stepped in, the panel glided shut, and the cab began to descend slowly.

It paused two stories down, and another panel slipped open without sound. And at that instant Operator 5 acted.

Both his hands shot out at the same instant, with the speed of light. One gripped the throat of the man at his left; the other struck a flashing, stiff-fingered blow to the forehead of the second. The first grabbed at his gun, but abandoned the move to tear at Operator 5's tendoned wrist with both hands. The other tottered stiffly against the side of the cab, dazed by the jiu-jitsu attack. Jimmy Christopher whirled and struck again—a dazing blow which staggered the first backward.

He sprang out of the car and touched the starter button as he whirled away. The cab began to slide upward, while the panel remained open. One of the two undercover agents remained stiffly toppled against the wall of the car, while the other scrambled madly to escape it through the narrowing opening. He jerked back as the space closed, and as Jimmy Christopher sped along a narrow corridor to a secret door beyond which lay freedom.

His touch on a concealed button opened the way. He stepped

into a closet; pushed through an opening into the steamy, greasy kitchen of a restaurant. Then he hurried along the counter at the front and into the street.

He knew his attack on the two men would mean only a moment's delay; that a warning would flash in a few seconds over all Washington.

Swift strides carried him to an Intelligence car parked at the curb. Scrambling inside, he sent it forward sharply and around a corner. Glancing back, he saw gleaming headlights swing away from the front of the restaurant. He pressed his motor to the limit, striving to lose himself in the maze of radiating and encircling streets.

CHAPTER 8
SECRET MAN-HUNT

TIM DONOVAN huddled in the blackness of the doorway, a shadow in the gloom filling the remote extremity of Avenue X. He had kept a long, tireless vigil under the orders of Operator 5. Not once during his waking moments had he relaxed his watch of the strange house numbered 2700. He was hungry, worn—but alert.

His eyes brightened as a car purred along the street; clouded with disappointment as it passed. Again he turned his aching eyes toward the suspicious house; and his alertness tightened as he saw a dark figure nearing it.

A man who was a mere shadow in the gloom approached the entrance of the building. At the steps he paused and glanced around swiftly, furtively. He hurried to the entrance; melted through.

There were now four men and a woman in the house, Tim Donovan knew—and one of the men was the secret agent who had attempted to scuttle Jimmy Christopher's power-boat. Each passing moment strained at the tough little Irish lad's nerves—until a quick step on the pavement startled him.

A smart, erect figure strode past. Tim Donovan whispered an exclamation: "Jimmy!" Immediately the passerby whirled and blended into the shadow beside the boy. "Gee, Jimmy—that was you in the car after all! Somebody else has just gone in!"

"Steady, old timer!" Operator 5 cautioned. "Before we go a step farther, I've got to warn you that the Intelligence is hunting for me. I was made a prisoner of war, and I broke away!"

"Gee, Jimmy! That's imp—"

"It's true, Tim. If I'm caught now, and you're with me, you'll be taken prisoner too. It's a chance. You'd better slip away and let me handle this alone."

"No, Jimmy!" the boy protested, wide-eyed. "No matter what happens, I'm sticking with you!"

Operator 5 smiled tightly. "Good boy, Tim. I know you'd say that. I need your help. If you'll run the chance with me, Tim—"

"Count on me, Jimmy!"

"I've got to get inside that house. I want you to get closer, and keep watching it. A car chased me from WDC-13—it might trail me here. If you see any Intelligence men show up, knock on the door of 2700. Three loud quick raps, then two."

"Sure, Jimmy!"

"Watch sharp!"

Operator 5 slipped out of the doorway and hurried to the corner. He felt an uncanny sensation of eyes watching him— eyes other than those of Tim Donovan. He turned into the side street and near the rear of the house flattened against a black wall. Peering back, he saw Tim Donovan dart across the street and vanish. The boy was taking his closer position.

Reaching up, Operator 5 gripped the top of the wall, drew himself to a crouching position on it. He poised gingerly, feeling the sharp teeth of jagged glass—and again he sensed hidden eyes watching him. He dropped down into thick darkness, and peered at the house. Its every window was black.

HE DRIFTED to the rear door and found it stoutly barred. Clinging to a post of the porch, he climbed and, once on the sloping roof, tried two windows. Both were caught. Quickly he slipped from his pocket a flat tool, its one end thinned in a fishtail edge. With the utmost care he pried it into a crack of a sash and bore down. At each creak of the withdrawing screws he stiffened and listened. But he persisted until the catch came free.

He slipped over the sill, bringing out his automatic. A ringing silence filled the darkness of the room he entered. He eased into an uncarpeted hallway, and the silence still held. He mounted a flight of stairs, testing each step as he climbed. In the third floor hallway he directed his noiseless steps to a closed door. In the center of the hallway he paused, hearing faint, guttural voices.

"… way to the Canal will be opened. It is only a matter of hours. Any move the U.S. generals make will play into our hands!"

"There is no danger? With Operator 5 working against us—and still alive—"

A chesty chuckle sounded, "He's already marked himself as a traitor. His own service will eliminate him from the scene of action. He knows much—he's dangerous—but I've taken many steps to make sure the United States itself renders him helpless for us!"

"Perhaps he's told of this place! It's dangerous to come here when—"

"Tonight," the guttural tones interrupted again, "we are using this place for the last time. We shall—"

Somewhere beyond a bell clanged once, and the sound vibrated into silence.

Operator 5 poised. The note of the small gong froze his blood. Had he unconsciously tripped an alarm, in some way betrayed his presence to those in the room beyond? Uncertainty held him motionless as he leveled his automatic at the door.

For a long moment he stood, listening into silence. But it was as if he had heard words spoken by specters, who had melted into nothingness at the tone of the bell.

He stepped forward tensely. His hand stole through the dark to the door behind which had sounded the voices. Noiselessly he twisted it. His steady, slow pressure opened it a crack. He saw only darkness beyond, listened into silence.

Had those in the room slipped away? Or were they waiting for a repetition of the alarm, which evidently had signaled a hostile presence in the house? Grimly, Operator 5 stepped into the thick blackness beyond the door.

119

Suddenly—blinding light!

The glare shot from overhead. His stinging eyes glimpsed a startling sight as he instinctively leaped aside. Against the far wall, men and women stood in a line, facing him. One woman with skin of a yellowish tint was huddled fearfully in the corner. Three men were half crouched, guns leveled. Beside them stood a huge man, his face masked in black.

"Operator 5!" rang sharply from the masked man's heavy lips. INTO THE blurted name the guns blasted. Bullets crashed across the room, splintering into the wall beside him as he side-leaped. His own automatic spat a swift echo. Three times he sent slugs cracking at the huddled figures. A fourth time he fired, and his shot shattered into the blinding bulbs overhead.

Darkness filled the room as he sprang aside. The guns of the espionage agents sent a withering fusillade at him. It was a savage, murderous burst that stopped abruptly. Then, into the ringing silence, came a dull, resounding concussion. Again fragments of glass tinkled. A misty dampness filled the air around Jimmy Christopher, a stinging pungency bit into his lungs.

Instantly he knew that a gas bomb had been hurled at him; that it was gusting lethal fumes into the air.

Again he sprang aside, snatching the little silver case from his pocket. Deftly he removed two of the impregnated porcelain wafers from it and slipped them into his nostrils. He heard quick movements during that tense moment, and knew that the others were darting from the room. Once he was breathing through the filters, he crept along the wall, flicking on his electric torch.

A strangling cry came out of the gloom as the thin beam shot across the room. The light played upon a window, and he saw the yellow-skinned woman opening it and clambering frantically over the sill. The espionage agents, in their haste to escape the deadly fumes in the room, had bolted the door upon the girl and trapped her.

Operator 5 shouted a sharp warning, and sprang to seize her arm. She turned terrified eyes upon him. The torture of the gas contorted her face and greater terror filled her as she tore free and jumped. He leaned out through the window and looked down. The girl lay motionless, sprawled on the cement walk below.

His eyes glittered dark in the shine of his torch as he darted toward the door which connected with the room into which the four men had fled. The way was bolted.

Turning back, he saw a metal cabinet standing against the wall, its face a mosaic of small, steel doors, each numbered, each slitted for a key. They were lock-boxes. They meant that this house was a "cover address" for the espionage ring, that here spies came to receive orders left in their boxes for them. Giving the bank of locked compartments only a glance, Operator 5 sprang into the hallway. His swinging beam lighted its emptiness.

Hearing quick footfalls below he started to the head of the stairs—and stopped short as a new sound shocked through the tense stillness. Three sharp raps—then two. The signal of Tim Donovan, warning that Intelligence men were nearing the house.

He ran down the stairs, darted to the front entrance. Seeing the shadow of a head on the pebbled pane, he quickly drew the bolt and Tim Donovan, at his command, slipped in.

"Jimmy! Four men coming—Intelligence men!"

"Stick close, Tim!"

OPERATOR 5 whirled back, and the tough little Irish lad hurried at his side. Standing open beneath the lowest flight of stairs was a door through which damp air gusted. It led into a cellar. His light gleamed before him, Operator 5 started down. And then he paused, as the beam covered a still figure lying at the bottom—a man whose wide eyes were glazed in death. He knew one of his own bullets had done that.

He sped down, and again jerked to a stop. A rustle of movement in the gloom warned him. Suddenly two swift shots cracked out of a far corner; two slugs hissed past his head. The beam of his torch cut into the darkness, and he fired as the light brought into relief a face that was a mask of agony.

Red blood glistened in the white shaft and the espionage agent who was huddled in the corner now lurched down. Operator 5 sprang toward him, saw that the hand holding a gun was limp in death, and grimly turned away. His light led him to an iron door in the side wall. He gripped its handle and tugged with all his strength, but it gave not the slightest fraction of an inch.

"They've gotten out that way, Tim! They're escaping through the next house! We—"

He broke off as a loud hammering sounded above. "The Intelligence agents!"

"Quick, Tim! After me! They'll be all around the house in a minute!"

He sprang up the basement stairs with the Irish lad at his heels. Shadows were moving on the pane, at the front entrance. As they sprang to the rear entrance, a swinging gun butt cracked the front glass. They darted into the darkness of the walled yard, sprang to the corner of the house, peered around it. Along the cement walk there was no movement, no sign of people save the still figure of the gassed girl.

Operator 5 hurried to her side. One glance told him the plunge had instantly killed her. He played his light an instant into her face; her features registered with photographic clarity on his memory. His hand shot out to pick up the purse she had dropped, and he whirled back.

Heavy steps sounded inside the house as the Intelligence men hurriedly searched the rooms.

He bounded across the enclosed yard, signaling Tim Donovan to come after him. At the inner wall he hoisted the boy up. Tim scrambled gingerly over the glass on top of the wall, then Operator 5 climbed also. One of his hands became covered with red as he poised and dropped. With Tim Donovan at his side he scurried across the adjacent yard. Darkness lay thick along the way they fled....

Z-7 JERKED up from his desk as Operator S-8 strode swiftly into the inner office of WDC-13. S-8 was one of the two men who had been ordered to imprison Operator 5. He was the man who had trailed Jimmy Christopher to the "cover address" of the espionage ring. His jaw clamped hard, his eyes glittered as he strode to the desk of the Washington chief.

"Operator 5?" Z-7 demanded. "He—"

"No sign of him, Chief! No report from the men searching for him since I phoned you." He pushed a packet of typewritten documents across the desk. "Look those over! So far as Operator 5 goes—they settle him once and for all!"

Z-7 unfolded the documents and stared at them.

"I found keys on both the dead men in that place. One was a master key to the lock-boxes in the upper room. I searched the whole bank. Those papers were in one of the compartments. They speak for themselves!"

Z-7 sank into his chair, stunned, staring at the pages. His face went white. His stubby fingers trembled. He glared up at the grim S-8.

"This—this is a record of payments made to Operator 5 by the Yellow Espionage office! These papers show that Operator 5 has sold out to the enemy! Good God—I can't believe he's turned traitor for mere money!"

"Those figures are plenty high, Chief! Every man has his price. That explains everything, doesn't it? It shows why he opened the way for the Yellow invasion, why he tried to incite mutiny in the Army and Navy! *He sold out!*"

Z-7's ebon eyes glittered like smouldering coal. He touched a button on his desk. The chief dispatcher hurried from the clattering communications room. The Washington chief, his fist clenched, snapped, "Orders!"

Over the secret web of teletype and telephone wires radiating from WDC-13 the unprecedented orders flashed. To every Intelligence headquarters outside the invaded zone, to every undercover agent in the service, the grim word reached.

ARREST OPERATOR 5 ON SIGHT—CONSIDERED MOST DANGEROUS ENEMY OF THE UNITED STATES—WDC-13.

As the urgent orders spread, a power-boat skirted through the thick darkness along the banks of the Potomac. It stole into Chesapeake Bay, into the open Atlantic. Eyes alert, Tim Donovan huddled in the gloom beside Operator 5, who, a fugitive hunted by the government he served, guided its furtive course through the blackness of the night....

CHAPTER 9
FOUR FOR COUNTRY

TERRIFIED NEW York listened to shrieking newsboys running through the streets, stared at the startling headlines which blackened each new extra edition that came in tides from the few great presses which Yellow sabotage had not wrecked.

YELLOW FLEET STEAMING CLOSE TO PANAMA!
U.S. NAVY RUSHING TO BLOCK CANAL!
SEA BATTLE IMMINENT!
INVISIBLE POWER MOWS DOWN U.S. ARMY!

Though newsboys howled the startling developments as they scurried past the front of a staid apartment building in the Sixties just off Central Park, the feeble old man who alighted from the cab paid no attention. He shuffled on bent legs to the entrance, tugging a muffler close around his wizened face.

He paused when the doorman opened the door for him and asked:

"Who do you wish to see, sir?"

"Mr. Huntley Walsh," the old man cackled. "Mr. Walsh, on the eleventh floor. He's expecting me."

An elevator carried the unsteady ancient to the eleventh floor. When the cab dropped out of sight, however, his manner quickened. He slipped a key from his pocket to unlock a door—a door of steel, veneered with mahogany. Once inside, his sagged shoulders squared, he straightened alertly, flung off coat and muffler. In an instant he became the young man whom the doorman knew as Huntley Walsh!

He stepped into the bathroom and vigorously scrubbed make-up stain from his face. He changed his baggy, threadbare suit for one smartly tailored. A few moments, and his appearance was utterly changed. His maid, had she been present, would have addressed him as Mr. Walsh—she did not know his real name was James Christopher.

In the adjoining room, he swung an anchored table toward the window. Bolted to it was a strange contrivance which consisted of a ratcheted drum, a powerful electric motor and a long, flexible gooseneck to which was attached a box like a camera—a lens looking from its one end.

Uncoiling forty feet of rope ladder from the drum, he slipped it over the sill, and climbed upon it, descending into the darkness of a passageway which separated the one building from the next. He swung to a balcony on the adjacent apartment house, drew his torch from his pocket, shot its beam upward. The photoelec-

126

tric cell in the projecting black box activated a relay, the motor in the room above whirred, the rope ladder slid upward, and the window uncannily closed.

Operator 5 walked through an apartment he had rented under the name of Morton Clegg, stepped into the hallway and at another door pushed a button inscribed *Carleton Victor.* It was opened by a cool faced manservant who bowed and said:

"Good evening, Mr. Victor."

THE ESTIMABLE Crowe, gentleman's gentleman extraordinary, was utterly unaware that the identity of Carleton Victor, photo-portraitist of worldwide reputation, was a convenient mask for the undercover operations of Jimmy Christopher. Victor, who maintained sumptuous studios on Fifth Avenue, was the most sought after photographer in the metropolis. The great of the world were flattered by the favor of his lens, and his signature on a photo-portrait was in itself a credential of importance. None of his eminent sitters dreamed that Carleton Victor was in reality Operator 5 of the United States Intelligence— now an escaped prisoner of war.

Z-7 alone, in the service, knew of Operator 5's covering identity; Z-7 knew the address of Victor's sumptuous penthouse. The Washington chief did not know, however, Operator 5's secret means of entering the apartment—a means cleverly devised to throw off any possible trailers who might discover that Victor and Operator 5 were one.

"I trust you had a pleasant journey to Washington, sir—and a restful one?" Crowe continued.

Victor smiled wryly. "An interesting one, Crowe. My return trip, too, was one I shall long remember."

Giving over his Homburg and stick he opened the door of a closet and stepped in. Once past the sill, Carleton Victor ceased to exist and Operator 5 returned.

The closet contained nothing but a telephone, and was completely soundproofed. Jimmy Christopher brought it into use at once, and called the number of a house designated in the lexicon of the Intelligence as Address Y.

Immediately a girl's voice answered.

"Di!" Operator 5 exclaimed. "Lord, it's good to hear your voice again! Is Tim there—and safe?"

"Yes, Jimmy!" Diane Elliot answered breathlessly. "I thought I'd never hear from you. Tim's told me everything. I'm terribly worried, Jimmy—what can you do?"

"Perhaps," Operator 5 answered, "nothing. But I'm going to try my best. As long as I can stay free, I'll not stop working on this case. Di, ask Tim—"

"But, Jimmy! It's so unfair! If they catch you it will mean—oh, Jimmy, you'll be thrown into prison, at least for the duration of the war—and if the Yellow forces invade the whole country and defeat us, it means you'll be kept a prisoner for life!"

"I know, Di," Operator 5 answered tightly. "That at the least. There's still a chance of coming through. It's a million to one gamble, but—it's got to be played. Di, I want you to stay there with Dad. Has Tim been watching the street?"

"He has, Jimmy! He's seen several Intelligence men outside.

They're watching this place. They'll arrest you if you try to come here!"

"And they'll trail you if you leave," Operator 5 told the girl tightly, "on the chance you'll lead them to me. This place is being watched too; I made sure of that before I came in. I have a plan, but—wait for me, Di!"

"Jimmy, please—please be careful!"

OPERATOR 5'S eyes narrowed in thought as he turned from the telephone. He pushed open the door, and it was as Carleton Victor that he emerged, to eye the waiting Crowe calculatingly. "Crowe," he said suddenly, "I have a highly unusual request to make of you. Don't question me, but do as I say."

"Yes, sir?" Crowe asked calmly.

He opened the door of another closet; removed a topcoat of smart pattern, a fine derby, a gay scarf. At his directions the amazed Crowe got into them. He passed Crowe his stick and finally brought out a morocco leather case on which the golden initials C.V. were stamped.

"Your instructions, Crowe, are simple. Go down in the elevator, and out the entrance. Keep your hat pulled low and your scarf pulled high. Carry the case so that the initials plainly show. Walk up the avenue three blocks, cross west one block, and immediately return. You understand that?"

"No, sir—er, yes, sir," Crowe answered with a blink. "Your choice of pattern, sir, if I may say so, sir, is a little—let us say—a little too happy for me, sir, but if you direct me to, sir—"

"I do, Crowe—and hurry! Do exactly as I have said, and start now."

The bewildered Crowe opened the door. He was aware that his unaccustomed garb lent him a marked resemblance to Carleton Victor, but this fact only increased his bewilderment. He stepped out and, on sudden thought, turned back.

"Beg pardon, sir," he said. "Your remarkable request almost made me forget a matter of importance. If I may, sir, I should like to take a holiday."

"A holiday, Crowe? Never before as long as you've been with me, have you asked for a holiday."

"No, sir," Crowe admitted. "You see, sir, I have a sister. She's asked me to visit her, sir, and I feel that I should. If you don't mind, sir, I should like to have several weeks for the purpose. It's going to be a family reunion, of a sort, sir."

"I never imagined, Crowe, that a man like you could be capable of possessing relatives. For that matter, I can't picture you eating, sleeping, or behaving like an ordinary person at all. You are such a perfect manservant, Crowe, that you can't possibly be anything else besides. Where does your sister live?"

"Thank you, sir. Very much, sir," Crowe said. "In Los Angeles, sir."

Carleton Victor started. *"Where?"*

Very apologetically Crowe repeated: "In Los Angeles, sir, if you don't mind."

Carleton Victor grew stern. "Crowe, you're persisting in your abominable habit of never reading the newspapers! Good God, man! You unnerve me! You want to take a holiday in Los Angeles, indeed!"

Crowe became perceptibly deflated. "I did, sir," he said meekly.

"For excellent reasons, Crowe, I flatly refuse your request. You may *not* take a holiday in Los Angeles. I'm doing it for your own good, understand. If you attempted it you'd find yourself in most distressing circumstances and—well, never mind. Since you never read the newspapers, you'd only be bewildered if I explained."

"Very good, sir," Crowe murmured. "Ah—I shall go now?"

"Certainly! Go at once!"

"Like—ah—this, sir?'

"Exactly as you are! One thing more, Crowe. If you are, let us say, suddenly set upon, don't be alarmed. Take it as a matter of course. Don't allow it to ruffle your admirable calm."

"No, sir," Crowe whispered in complete bewilderment. "Very good, sir. Is there anything else, sir?"

"Nothing remains, Crowe, except for you to start."

"Yes, sir."

RELUCTANTLY CROWE closed the door. Confusion teemed in his usually ordered mind as he waited for the arrival of the lift. The elevator attendant stared at him in amazement while he descended, and Crowe's pointed nose twitched in embarrassment. He hurried out the entrance, avoided the gleeful eyes of the doorman, and began the mysterious round appointed him by his master.

Victor's brilliant scarf. Victor's form fitting topcoat, Victor's jaunty derby all contributed to an acute distress. The fact that he was carrying one of Victor's precious cameras made him step as gingerly as though he had a new-born babe in his arms. But, flawless manservant that he was, he obeyed orders to the letter; kept his face in shadow and followed the strange route laid down for him.

It was not until he was again approaching the entrance of the apartment house that he was, in the words of Carleton Victor, suddenly "set upon." Two men sprang toward him, blocking his path. Another straddled behind him. He became too startled even to gasp when he discovered that they were leveling automatics at him. He stood and stared—and quaked.

Suddenly he felt Victor's derby snapped back, Victor's scarf jerked down. He saw amazement jerk into the faces of the men with the guns. He heard one of them gasp: "That's not him!" His dumbfoundment increased as the three whirled and left him standing alone, utterly unharmed.

"I say!" he exclaimed.

He saw them hurry into the lobby of the apartment house as a uniformed messenger boy emerged. He hastened after them, but found them gone. When at last he reached the penthouse level he saw the door of his master's apartment standing wide open and the three engaged in searching it. He advanced, now fortified by the security of his position, and declared:

"You gentlemen must leave at once, or I shall call the police!"

The three peered at each other incredulously. One of them advanced and shook a stern finger under Crowe's aristocratic nose. "Where is he?" the man demanded. "Open up! Where is he?"

"If you are referring to Mr. Victor," Crowe answered with stiff dignity, "he was here a moment ago but now, obviously, he has gone."

It was indeed obvious that Carleton Victor was gone. The three Intelligence men glared at Crowe, tramped out the door, and slammed it. The estimable manservant seized the opportunity to divest himself immediately of Victor's coat and scarf and hat. He strode from empty room to empty room, returned to the door, and looked about in a daze.

"Where on earth," he asked himself aloud, "did Mr. Victor go?"

He did not dream that the messenger boy, who had slipped out the entrance at the very moment the Intelligence men were entering the building, was the man known as Carleton Victor—in reality, Operator 5.

THE HOUSE designated Address Y in the secret lexicon of the U.S. Intelligence was a modest brownstone front in the east forties in Manhattan. It was the home of John Christopher, the father of Operator 5, once designated Operator Q-6, and it was also the home of Tim Donovan. As the loyal Irish lad waited for further word from Jimmy Christopher, following the telephone call that Diane Elliot had received, he huddled at a dark window and peered through the crack of the drawn blind.

In the gloom of the street below he had already spotted Intelligence men watching the house. He saw furtive movements now. They were acting under orders relayed from WDC-13, Tim knew, and his heart pounded with anxiety as he turned back, passed through a door, and returned to the lighted living-room.

"Gee, Di!" he exclaimed. "Maybe they've found Jimmy already! If they grab him again, he'll never have another chance to get away!"

Diane Elliot's eyes were dark with worry. She peered at the mild-mannered man who was moving nervously about the living-room.

John Christopher felt unbounded admiration for his son. He himself had been forced from the Intelligence Service by a wound which still constantly endangered his life. Two bullets lay so close to the vital nerve centers of his heart that no surgeon dared attempt to remove them. He was forced to live a life of quiet; any sudden excitement could have meant his death. And, denied active service, he gloried in the achievements of Operator 5. But now the blot on his son's name caused him deep concern. His eyes were haggard, his mouth drawn; he had to force a smile as Diane Elliot came to him.

"I know Jimmy's right!" the girl declared staunchly. "No matter what anyone else says or thinks of Jimmy Christopher, I'll believe in him!"

"Gee, Di!" Tim Donovan exclaimed. "Jimmy's the only one who realizes the truth—and he can't make anyone else see it! Not even Z-7 suspects the spy ring that's operating isn't a Yellow ring at all! Jimmy's sure of it. He told me that it's headed by an American, that most of the espionage agents are Americans. He's certain the Yellow invasion was planned with the help of that spy ring in this country. He's told me how the Yellowese espionage system works in Asia—but this ring is under a different leader."

John Christopher spoke quietly. "Di—Tim. We're all placed in a trying situation. I believe in Jimmy—so do you both, with all your heart. But he's a fugitive—he's being hunted—and the moment's coming when we must decide, once and for all, whether we—" He broke off quickly as a furtive sound came from the rear of the house.

Tim Donovan sprang at once to a door at the back of the room. He opened it upon the workshop of Operator 5—rooms cluttered with machinery, walls filled with shelves carrying strange devices the nature of which only Jimmy Christopher knew—and stared at the rear window. He saw a hand raising the sash. And he saw a face appear in the glow.

"Jimmy!" He leaped to the window; Diane Elliot and John Christopher followed.

OPERATOR 5 climbed in quickly. The girl flung her arms around him in a wild burst of joy, kissed him square on the lips; and he backed away in red faced confusion. Tim Donovan hugged him in glee, and ex-Operator Q-6 seized his hand.

He quickly drew the blind of the window down and strode into the living-room. He was now wearing a smartly tailored business suit. His eyes were shining with alertness.

"Lord, I'm being hunted all over the city!" he exclaimed. "I don't dare return to the penthouse, nor to the studio. I won't be able to come here again. Fortunately, I have several places in town where I can hide out. I came here to see you, Tim. And you, Di."

"Gee, Jimmy, you've got to watch yourself! It'll be all over if they find you!"

"I know, Tim. I've got to keep out of sight at all costs—but I'm not letting go of this case. I'm going to follow it through to the end—unless Z-7's men capture me first. I can't do it alone.

I've got to have help. There's no one else in the world I can turn to but you, Tim—and you, Di. And Dad—?"

"I'm with you, Jimmy!" Tim blurted.

Diane Elliot smiled. "Jimmy Christopher, you needn't even ask for whatever help I can give you. Just tell me what I can do."

John Christopher stood wordless, peering deep into his son's eyes. Operator 5 faced him solemnly.

"Dad, you can help too—but I'm not going to ask you to. The Service means everything to you. It would be too much to expect you to turn against the chief even for my sake. It would be a tremendous help to me if I could learn the plans of the Intelligence and the General Staff from the inside, but—"

"Son," ex-Operator Q-6 began tightly, "In this situation I can't—" He broke off as a bell jangled—a shrill warning that someone was at the street entrance.

Operator 5 turned sharply. He stepped to the wall, swung a small picture aside. Behind it, a brilliant lens was mounted flush with the wall. He brought his eye close to it. Through a tube that angled down in the walls, fitted with carefully arranged mirrors, he saw an image—men standing in the street. He saw one press the call button again, and again the bell shrilled.

Jimmy Christopher turned back quickly. "Z-7!" he exclaimed. "Perhaps he knows I'm in here! Dad—you've got to stay and see the chief. Tim, Di—after me!"

Operator 5 quickly passed a slip of paper to his father—a slip on which a cryptic number was written.

John Christopher watched in dismay as Operator 5 hurried again into the workshop. Diane snatched up coat and hat to follow; Tim Donovan pulled his broken billed cap on his head. They closed the door behind them as Jimmy Christopher raised the window.

He helped the girl out, Tim Donovan scrambled after her, and he himself sprang over the sill last. He closed the window, turned in the dark court, led them through deep shadow. He opened a gate in a wooden fence—a gate invisible to one who did not know it was there—and directed them to the rear of a building fronting on the next street. His key unlocked a door, he led them up two flights, admitted them with another key into dark rooms. The air was musty, as though this apartment had remained long closed.

The snap of a light switch disclosed a plain but comfortable bedroom. He stepped quickly into the adjoining room, where, in one corner, stood a black paneled box. Dials marked its gleaming front, a pair of headphones connected to their pin-jacks. Jimmy Christopher spoke quickly as he brought the phones to his head.

"This is one of my hideouts—I've had it ready for years," he said swiftly. "You know another, Tim—the place where the boat is hidden—but that's only part of it. These phones are connected with a microphone hidden in Dad's living-room." His hand moved to a switch and he paused, his eyes solemn. "Do you understand?" he asked. "If you help me, you'll make yourselves traitors in Z-7's eyes—you'll be in as much danger as I."

"It makes no difference to me whatever," Diane Elliot said. "That's my answer."

"I'd be sticking with you, Jimmy," Tim Donovan declared, "even if everybody in the whole world was against you!"

Operator 5 smiled slowly. "Nobody could ask for truer friends than you," he said softly. "With your help, there's a fighting chance—"

His voice faded, and a click echoed as he pressed the cam of the switch.

IMMEDIATELY A voice sounded in the phones—the voice of Z-7, speaking in the house of John Christopher.

"I know," the chief was saying, "how painful this is to you, Q-6. It's the toughest job I've ever faced—but I have no choice. There's only one possible move and I'm taking it. I'm trying in every way possible to make a prisoner of your son."

"I know, Chief," John Christopher's husky voice came over the wire. "You can't do anything else."

"It's far more serious than you believe, Q-6," Z-7's tones persisted. "He's involved under the 46th Article of War!" *

"The penalty for that—you know it may be—" Z-7 broke off raspingly. "These—these are photostats of documents we found at a cover-address in Washington being used by a ring of spies. They prove that Operator 5 is one of the Yellow espionage ring—that he sold out to the enemy. Do you understand that?" There was no answer from Operator Q-6.

---

* Author's Note: ARTICLES OF WAR: 46—"Whosoever holds correspondence with, or gives intelligence to, the enemy, either directly or indirectly, shall suffer death, or such other punishment as a court-martial may direct."

The rule of "non-intercourse" with the enemy governs all soldiers and citizens in time of war.

"I am obliged," Z-7 persisted in a tortured tone, "to put a cruel decision before you, Q-6. The Service needs men. In the emergency we must recall veteran operators like you. It not only involves a grave risk for you, but, if you consent to return to the Service—you are bound by your oath to help me capture Operator 5."

Q-6's voice crackled. "You're asking me to rejoin the Service? Now? God, Chief! It's a chance I'll gladly give my life for. But—"

"You must decide, here and now, once and for all," the edged voice of Z-7 continued, "whether you are to be loyal to the Service, or loyal to your son."

Jimmy Christopher listened intently through the long pause that followed. His blood beat hotly; he scarcely breathed. At last, so softly that the words were scarcely audible, the answer of John Christopher came over the secret wire.

"I am an Intelligence man, Chief, and an American. My vow pledges me—to do my utmost to preserve my country—against all dangers."

"Your son, Q-6, is such a danger."

"Yes. My son—is such a danger."

Operator 5 sat tense as the voices lowered. He heard movements which meant that his father was leaving the room with Z-7. Jimmy Christopher slipped off the earphones, and his eyes darkened deeply. He rose, stood motionless a moment, while the eyes of Tim Donovan and Diane Elliot clung to his and the color of his cheeks faded.

A strained cry sounded in the street—the voice of a newsboy shouting the latest extra edition as he ran. Operator 5 strode quickly to the window. He listened to screeching words that chilled him:

"U.S. Army retreating before Yellow advance!

"Thousands killed in new Yellow attacks!

"Invasion sweeps east, routing American Army!

"Yellow Fleet battling way to Panamá Canal!

"Terrific sea fight in bay of Panamá—fleets fighting for control of Canal!"

Operator 5 turned from the window, his eyes glinting, black as the night outside.

"The master strategy of the Yellow Command has begun!" he declared. "If it succeeds, the United States is doomed!"

CHAPTER 10
THE YELLOW POWER STRIKES

THE THUNDER and lightning of battle, even at that moment, rolled across the Bay of Panamá, as the fleets of two great powers fought.

The Atlantic and Pacific Fleets had drawn together in the bay. Directed by the orders of General Staff, they had plowed under full steam to block the entrance of the Panamá Canal against the swift approach of the Yellow Squadrons. Their funnels pouring, they had raced against time to take strategic positions. Hour by hour the clash had drawn nearer—and now the rumble and flash of battle tore at sea and sky.

From the flight decks of the airplane-carriers, *Saratoga* and *Ranger,* battle planes swarmed into a sky already blackened by the thunderous concussions of Yellow anti-aircraft batteries. The bay was churned by falling shells as the sea-monsters rocked out screaming devastation.

In the midst of the cosmic turmoil, Rear-Admiral Cartley, Commander of the combined fleets, stood on the open bridge of the battleship *Houston,* and through powerful binoculars peered at the tossing ships of his formation. Again and again the big guns struck across the heaving bay at the approaching Yellow Squadrons. Out of the howling sky dropped the projectiles of the enemy batteries, hurling their rending tons of steel and explosives upon the U.S. ships.

Yet it was not the crushing damage of the shells that most deeply concerned Admiral Cartley. It was a weighty dread that again, out of the depths of the night, the strange invisible power of the Yellow Command might strike.

And even as he waited its inevitable coming—it did strike!

Before his aching eyes he saw the glow appear and envelope the battleship *New York.* He saw the antenna wires shine first; saw the evil light spread further, over the entire ship; saw the crew run madly across smoking decks, behind gleaming rails, past guns that shone red hot, then white! Minute by minute the certainty of doom crept upon the *New York* while horrified officers watched from the bridge of the flagship—watched a great monster of war become another beacon of hell.

A crashing explosion blanketed the *New York* with flame. The sea boiled white where the mighty ship had rolled. Wind tore the smoke away to disclose water that steamed with the destructive heat playing invisibly through the night. And even

141

as the mist of destruction floated over the other great ships of the formation, the hellish glow appeared again, to envelope still another!

Swiftly the awesome power spread. Even while the cruiser *Portland* shone red hot in the waves, the battleship *Maryland* began to shine in the night. Even while the *Portland* became transformed into nothingness by the blasting power of her own exploding magazines, the destroyer *Wasmuth* took on the glow of doom. Again and again world-shaking concussions made the sea a whirlpool; again and again sizzling white metal rained from the sky; farther and farther along the U.S. formation the disintegrating force spread, promising doom to the entire combined fleet of the nation.

The horrified Admiral Cartley fought his way from the bridge, through lashing spray and tearing wind, to snap orders at his speechless officers.

"Order both fleets to withdraw southward! Order them to abandon formation! Get them out of this damned hell as fast as they can steam, any way they can travel! Withdraw them before the whole fleet plunges to the bottom of the bay!"

BEFORE THE devastating bolts of the invisible weapon of the Yellow Fleet, the gray monsters of the U.S. fled for their very existence. The smoke of their funnels made the night blacker as they abandoned their position. A decimated sea force plowed through waters sprinkled with the remains of airplanes knocked from the sky by that same dread power. Ignominiously they retreated, opening the way to the entrance of the Canal—and into that entrance the Yellow battle-monsters steamed.

Now the full strength of the Canal Zone defenses were flung by terrorized commanders upon the approaching ships of the enemy. Great cannons in concealed coast batteries barked and roared their defiance. Fighting planes leaped from the air bases of the Canal Zone to fling the power of their bombs against the looming attack. Against this moment all the fortifications of that narrow, vital lane of water had been erected, and now they went into concerted action against the approach of the enemy.

The power of the invisible Yellow force struck out of the night against the Canal Zone defenses. Airplanes plunged toward the enemy fleet—and into a hell of heat. Planes sizzled and shone in the air as they became trapped in the invisible, dread power. They whirled and plunged out of the air, their pilots abandoning ship without parachutes in their terror, or plunging to the sea engulfed in flames. Like a great, unseen spider-web, the invisible weapon struck down the fighting ships and cleared the air for a closer approach of the Yellow Squadron to the canal.

In the great cement abutments the big guns grew hot, red, then white. Men ran maddened while the force played upon them, arousing a stifling fever within their bodies, cooking their brains. Giant powder magazines became ovens; the ovens roared asunder as high-explosive unleashed its destructive force. From one defense unit to another the devastation spread, bringing turmoil and chaos beyond all control, leaving the sky filled with fumes and the earth smoking like a griddle. One by one the defensive units of the Panamá Canal were wiped away—and toward its entrance the ships of the Yellow Squadrons steamed.

Past the breakwaters and onto the shore small boats put out

from the swarming merchant marine behind the Yellow fleet swarming with Yellow soldiers. Their weapons found little to turn against as they herded into the Zone. The devastating play of the invisible power had opened the way for them, had left the most vulnerable link in the U.S. defenses open to easy seizure. While the Yellow ships hove to in the bay and waited, the Yellow scourge spread across the narrow isthmus, taking command.

Land wires carried the news of the appalling devastation to Washington, to New York, to every city in the nation. Millions read headlines that spelled doom to the United States. Thousands mobbed the streets to buy extra editions at exorbitant prices; while the ether was still "jammed" they read of the grim threat hovering now ever closer upon their homes and lives.

Even as they read, the Yellow blight was spreading from the west and rising in the east—the moment was approaching when the destiny of a great nation must be decided. Yellow or white! Democracy or imperial colony! Freedom, or slavery under a Yellow ruler! The answer was written in the coming hours.

Z-7, HIS face blackened by deep lines of exhaustion, strode stiffly to the office of Major-General Falk, Chief of Staff, in the building of the War Department, Washington. The air of the great edifice crackled with electrical tension. The quarters of the General Staff were filled with a frantic bustling. The Washington chief of the Intelligence heard the rasping voice of General Falk before he opened the door.

"The Yellow Command can be undertaking only one strategy! The Yellow Navy is advancing at this moment to bombard the eastern coast and open the way for their second invasion. The

Yellow merchant marine in the Atlantic is waiting even now to unload troops on our shore. The jaws of a trap are closing on us from both the east and the west!"

Z-7, pausing near the desperate officer, declared quietly: "I believe, General, that Operator 5 warned you of this at the very beginning!"

The officers of the General Staff glared at Z-7. The Secretary of War, rising from a chair, addressed an edged question to the chief.

"Have you found Operator 5, Z-7?"

"No. He is in New York—we are sure of that, but we haven't located him. We know now that he used a power-boat to escape from Washington to Manhattan, and I'm doing everything possible to locate that boat. It's only a matter of time until he becomes our prisoner."

"I advise you, sir," the Secretary of War declared stonily, "to make short work of it. Unless you do, you'll be removed from the Intelligence and a man put in your place who *is* equal to the task!"

Z-7's face went white with fury. "To that," he snapped, "I have nothing to say. I've come here to bring you important information. Here it is—a communication from Operator 5."

"What!" General Falk snapped. "You've heard from Operator 5 and you presume—"

"This information," Z-7 interrupted, "came to me through the mail. I'm attempting to trace the letter. Regardless of your opinion of Operator 5, gentlemen—read his information!"

The Secretary of War took the closely written pages, scanned them. He found with the letter pages torn from books and scientific periodicals. Z-7 spoke tersely while the Secretary read.

"Our government scientists have been absolutely unable to learn the nature of the invisible Yellow power—because those damned Yellow devils have taken pains to conceal it so well. Operator 5 has given us the first hint of the truth in these letters. Look at that scientific paper headed 'The Heating of Electrolytes in High-Frequency Fields.'* Read those recommendations of Operator 5 for protecting ourselves against the enemy power. That young man is, by all the evidence, a traitor to his country—but his advice cannot be ignored."

"And how," General Falk sneered, "does he say we may protect ourselves from that power?"

"He states that battleships, big guns, tanks, and such arma-

---

* AUTHOR's NOTE: The following is a transcript of the authoritative information given over by Operator 5 to Z-7. It may be found in *The Canadian Journal of Research*, volume 3, page 224: "The Heating of Electrolytes in High Frequency Fields," by J.C. McLennan, F.R.S., and A.C. Bunton, M.A. The report begins:

"Considerable interest has been aroused by the discovery that curious and unexpected physiological and biological effects are produced by short electromatic waves of wave-length 50 meters and under. Cosset, Cutwilst, Lakhowsky and Nagram, in 1924, reported an effect on plant tumors, while Schereschewsky, in 1926, noted a lethal effect on mice and inferred that certain wave-lengths had a specific effect on living cells. The production of fever in men has been observed. Later experiments show that the phenomenon observed so far can be explained as due to simple heating effects."

ments cannot be protected from it. Our only defense in these cases is to use the same power against the armaments of the enemy. Our one hope, he points out, is that—and defensive attack from the air. He outlines in his letter a means of rendering our airplanes invulnerable to the force.

"He states that non-metallic fuel tanks must be substituted for the usual equipment on our fighting planes. Bakelite, or glass and rubber tubing, must be used for the fuel lines. Non-metallic carburetors must be devised and put into use. Metal propellers must be discarded for wooden ones. Every bit of metal other than the motor itself must be stripped from the planes. They must carry their bombs submerged in containers of light oil."

GENERAL FALK snorted. "He believes that merely a bath of oil is sufficient to protect our shells and magazines?"

"He does. He states that powder-bags must be enclosed in cans and kept under oil—shells, bullets, small arms also. It's the only way of conserving our ammunition supply. You can trust that, gentlemen. The heat-force will play *through* the oil and heat the metal—it will certainly raise the oil to boiling point—but beyond the boiling point the temperature will not rise as long as the oil surrounds the hot metal. He names an oil with a boiling point lower than the detonation point of the explosive."

"And why," General Falk demanded, "is a traitor to the United States to be heeded at a time like this?"

"His recommendations are scientifically sound!" Z-7 declared. "Mr. Secretary, you must follow these stipulations. You must order these preparations made against the impending attack on our eastern coast!"

The Secretary of War glared at the Chief of Staff. "I shall have Operator 5's recommendations checked by our government scientists, and if they are not in error, I will order these changes made in our fighting equipment!"

"Useless!" Falk snapped. "Wars are not won with oil-baths and Bakelite tubing! The way to win a war is to fight the enemy down!"

"That is possible, General Falk," Z-7 declared, "only *if* we have armaments to fight with. Operator 5's purpose is to preserve them for that very purpose."

"That young man is a traitor! He can't be trusted! He's devised a new trap for us and by God, you're walking into it! I refuse—"

A sharp rap sounded on the door, and Falk growled a command. An adjutant hurried to him with dispatches. He glared at them, then peered at the Secretary.

"All our fortifications of the Canal Zone have been destroyed, all our men have been routed, and the Yellows have taken command. They're going to pass their naval squadrons through, into the Atlantic, at once. But, gentlemen, we hold the trumps in our hand. Some of our officers have reached Station M!"

The Secretary's eyes lighted. "They haven't been spotted by any of the Yellow agents in the Zone? They'll be able to make use of Station M?"

"Yes! We've hidden Station M well. Only a few know that we have the Canal mined against an emergency like this. Those men in Station M will be able to set off the hidden explosive and destroy the Canal—they'll be able to prevent the Yellow fleet from passing through! The destruction of the Canal from Station M will save us from invasion from the east!"

The Secretary grew pale. "It's true—setting off the mines, blocking the Canal, will stop the eastward passage of the Yellow Fleet. But—good God, gentlemen! We've done our best to preserve the Canal against sabotage and destruction by enemy agents, and now you propose we destroy it ourselves!" *

---

* AUTHOR'S NOTE: Recently Nelson Rounsevell, publisher of the *Panamá American,* declared that "twenty men, willing to risk their lives for their country, could blast the Panamá Canal to pieces in twelve hours and block the channel for a month." Army officials, commenting on the situation, said it would be impossible to prevent one person, carrying a small amount of high explosive, from slipping through the line of guards and doing great damage to a canal lock. The type of sabotage against which they said it would be almost impossible to guard would be the passage through the canal, from opposite ends, of two vessels heavily laden with mined explosives, to be exploded almost simultaneously when these vessels pass each other in the locks.

Another serious danger, according to army engineers, would be hostile aircraft. Fliers willing to sacrifice their lives might get close enough to the canal to dive at the locks with a plane loaded with explosives, and might succeed in putting the locks out of commission. To guard against such a possibility the War Department has planned to erect steel nets over each lock of the canal as soon as funds are available.

Officials believe the greatest danger to the canal is the possibility of damage to Gatun Dam. Recognizing this danger, War Department officials have placed extra strong guards around the structure.

"There is no other way, sir!" General Falk snapped. "We must block the Canal to stop the Yellow squadrons. If we don't, it means inevitable attack at our vital eastern defenses!"

Silence came into the room as the appalling step was considered. A chill pervaded Z-7's mind when he saw the Secretary of War nod. General Falk's words were rasping and sharp.

"Consult with the President, Mr. Secretary. Meanwhile, I'll flash orders to the officers hiding in Station M. I'll order them to hold themselves ready to set off the concealed mines and destroy the Canal when the Yellow fleet is passing through. It's the only way of saving ourselves from an utterly devastating onslaught in the east. My orders to wreck the Canal at the proper moment are going out at once!"

ON A corner of Times Square, New York—"the crossroads of the world"—a grimy faced, ragged newsboy gripped a bundle of newspapers under one arm as he shouted the latest startling headlines.

"Yellow Fleet preparing to steam through Canal!

"Invading ships about to pass into Atlantic!

"Entire east fears new attack!

"New York threatened by Yellow invasion!"

Scores bought papers from the dirty faced lad and hurried on. One who approached him was wearing the uniform of a New York City policeman. The young cop took a paper, passed the boy a coin, and turned away. Abruptly the youngster left his post, scurried into a drugstore, then a phone booth, and examined the coin given him by the policeman.

It was a shell of paper-thin metal, a slitted opening in one curved side. From the narrow slot the boy drew a bit of finest tissue paper. He unfolded it and read: *B at once*—5. He tore the message to bits, hurried into the street, and darted away.

Tim Donovan—the newsboy—had received an urgent message from Operator 5—the policeman—appointing an immediate, secret rendezvous.

IN THE office of the Metropolitan Nurse's Registry the telephone shrilled. The kindly faced woman at the desk answered the summons, made notes on a pad, and nodded.

"Miss Blake's here," she said. "I'll send her at once."

Miss Blake, in starched white nurse's uniform, came from a chair at the side of the room. The white-haired woman at the desk handed her a slip.

"Tubercular patient," Miss Blake was told, "at this address. The woman asked especially for you. Hurry right over—and good luck."

Miss Blake smiled her pleasure, took the slip and hastened from the registry office. Once in the street, she stepped into a taxi. The address she gave the driver was not that written on her appointment slip. It sent the cab scurrying far into the eastside.

Miss Blake was not hurrying to a patient's bedside. Diane Elliot was hastening to keep a secret rendezvous with Operator 5.

A SHADED globe played upon the head and shoulders of Jimmy Christopher as he bent tensely over the table. Amid a quiet broken only by the soft lapping of water behind him, he examined the contents of a purse. It was that of the woman spy who had plunged to her death from the third story window of the house at 2700 Avenue X, Washington.

Operator 5 removed, from the lining of the purse where it had been concealed, a small, red-backed book. It appeared to be a passport; its printing was in Yellowese characters. Quickly, working with pad and pencil, he discovered the inscriptions to be in code. He concentrated on the task of solving the puzzle of the secret writing; and when he straightened he knew that the booklet identified the dead woman as an agent of the Yellow espionage office.

He studied a small sheet, closely written with Yellowese, and again tackled the decipherment of a code. Labouredly, character by character, he penetrated its secret. His translation lengthened on his pad:

Agent 77, instructions. 25th, 12 midnight 156, Hudson, Shark. Duty aboard headquarters yacht, communications. Urgent to coördination of strategy.

OPERATOR 5 rose tensely, peering about through the gloom. This damp, moldering wharf-house, squatting on the western border of the East River in Manhattan, was his most carefully guarded hideout. On the dark water inside the shed his power-boat rocked gently.

A knock turned him to a door in the brick wall. He heard a signal rap repeated, drew the bolt, and Tim Donovan slipped in. The Irish lad's grimy face was lined with worry as he tossed his bundle of papers aside and strode with Operator 5 to a connecting door. They stepped into a small room, and a bright bulb snapped on.

"Jimmy! Nobody's spotted this place?" the boy asked anxiously.

"Not yet, Tim—but there are Intelligence men looking for my boat. Di's coming—we're waiting for her."

The room was walled with cabinets; every corner was cluttered. A telephone, a short-wave wireless installation, closets crowded with clothing for purposes of disguise—every conceivable accoutrement necessary to Operator 5 in his dangerous undercover activities. He had kept this hideaway a strict secret; not even Tim Donovan and Diane Elliot had known of it until he had led them to it.

He glanced at his watch uneasily, moved nervously about the room. Tim Donovan said anxiously.

"Gee, Jimmy—don't let it get you! Di'll be here in a minute. Take it easy. Jimmy—" his voice became pleading—"how about showing me a new trick?"

Operator 5 smiled. "Good idea, Tim. It'll be a simple one this time, while we wait. Watch me carefully now—I'm going to fool you completely."

Operator 5's tension eased as he brought an old hat from a closet. He showed Tim it was empty. Then, from his pocket, he drew two small cards.

"See here, old timer. This card is red—both sides—the other is plain white. I simply drop the two cards in this hat. Now, Tim, I'm about to make one of these cards fly through space without you even seeing it. Suppose you choose one of the colors."

"Red, Jimmy," the boy decided promptly while his eyes sparkled with eagerness.

"Okay, Tim. Red it is. I take the red card from the hat. There you are. Now I simply tuck it into my coat pocket. All right so far? The red card is in my pocket, and the white card is in the hat—isn't that so?"

"Sure!" Tim exclaimed.

"No, Tim, I'm afraid you're mistaken!" Operator 5 chuckled. "Here, in the hat, is the red card, not the white!" To the boy's amazement he lifted a red card from the hat and carefully laid it on the table. "And here, in my pocket is the white card, not the red!" From his pocket he drew the white card and placed it alongside the red on the table. "And there you are—the two cards changed places in the twinkling of an eye!"

"Tim blurted: "Gee! I was watching you pretty closely, Jimmy! You didn't make one tricky move—but they changed places all right!" He picked up the two cards, examined them minutely, and found nothing at all suspicious about them. "Gosh, how'd you do it?"

"Perhaps I'll have time to explain it before Di arrives, Tim," Operator 5 said with a smile. "It's very simple, and you can do it anywhere, any time—yet it's baffling. The whole secret is in the use of a third card—a card that's red on one side and white on the other."

OPERATOR 5 drew the trick card, which had differing colors on its two sides, from his pocket and displayed it.

"The success of the trick lies in its presentation, Tim. Follow this very carefully. When you start, have the all white card in

154

your left coat pocket. Have the all red card and the red-and-white card both in your right pocket. First, show the hat entirely empty. Stand with your left side to the spectator. Remove the two cards from your right pocket and hold them up—the thumb in front. You show the red card, and the red-and-white card with the *white* side showing, together.

"Casually show both sides of the red card. The spectator will naturally assume that the white card is an ordinary one, but you don't show him the rear side of it. You raise the hat, putting in the two cards. Then the spectator chooses one of the two colors. If he says 'red', you say 'I'll remove the red card.' If he says 'white', you say 'I'll leave the white card in the hat.' It comes to the same thing, either way. The spectator thinks he has made a choice, but he actually hasn't. Got it?"

"You fooled me there, Jimmy!" Tim exclaimed.

"Then," Operator 5 continued briskly, "you remove the red-and-white card from the hat, turning it so that the *red* side shows. Get that clear in your mind. You leave the all red card in the hat, you take out the red-and-white card with the red side showing, and you say 'the white card is left in the hat.' That shows, Tim, you can't believe anything a magician says!"

"I guess that's right, Jimmy!"

"Then, keeping the red side of the red-and-white card showing, you tuck it into your left coat pocket. Zip—and the magical change is made! You show that the red card, not the white, is in the hat. And from the pocket you remove the white card, not the red. When you show them this time, you handle them suspiciously, deliberately making the spectator think something's crooked about the cards. Then he picks them up and discovers nothing whatever wrong with them. The trick card remains in your pocket. There you are, Tim—simple and very effective!"

"Gee, Jimmy, that's swell!" Tim exclaimed. "I can buy the three kinds of cardboard at any stationery store, can't I? Or I can use ordinary white cards, and color two of them with red ink or red crayon!"

"Certainly Tim. In that case, you color both sides of one white card, and only one side of the second, and leave the third all white. Then you're all set. The spectator never suspects you use a third card, and the trick is so simple and so lacking in apparent trickery that you'll have your man guessing every time."

"Thanks, Jimmy! I'm going to practice that one and—"

A SOFT knock sounded in the wharf house beyond. Quickly Operator 5 slipped into the gloom. Tim Donovan waited anxiously as footfalls approached. When the door opened again Diane Elliot, wide-eyed, her color high in contrast to the starched white of her nurse's uniform, stepped into the light with Jimmy Christopher.

"I'm so glad you sent word at last, Jimmy!" she exclaimed. "If only I could do something to help—"

"You can, Di," Operator 5 declared. "It's a dangerous job, but an important one. If possible, I must learn the identity of the leader of the American espionage ring that is working for the Yellow War Office. I've got an important lead, but I can't follow it myself. Only you can do that. It involves a dangerous chance, Di."

"Let me try, Jimmy!"

"Good girl! Listen. I have the identification papers of a Yellowese-American girl, and her instructions. The coded orders direct her to go to Pier 156, at midnight tonight. There she is to board a waiting boat called the *Shark*. It's to carry her to a yacht, somewhere on the open sea, which is the headquarters of the leader of the Yellow-American spy ring. She is needed in the communications unit. Di—I want you to become that woman, Agent 77."

"I'll do it, Jimmy!"

"You know, Di—" Operator 5's voice became solemn—"if you're discovered it will mean the penalty of a spy operating in time of war—death."

Diane Elliot's eyes flashed. "It's not long until midnight now. I'll have to hurry."

"Good girl!" Operator 5 applauded her again. "Sit here!"

She took a chair in front of a mirror in the corner, Operator 5 brought from a drawer bottles of skin stain, tissue-thin fish skin, spirit gum, pigment crayons of the finest grade. Immediately, spreading a towel beneath the girl's chin, he went to work.

Carefully he applied stain that erased her high color. He applied invisible fish-skin to give her eyes an almond cast. He changed the shape of her mouth with carmine pencils, the whole shape of her face with more fish-skin and ingenious shading. Bit by bit Diane Elliot's features lost their American characteristics, and became oriental.

She made no protest when he applied dye that blackened her hair. He affixed false eye lashes with the utmost care, changed the shape of her nose by inserting thin silver tubes in her nostrils, gave a fullness to her face by small rolls of cotton tucked inside the cheeks. Under the light, a magical transformation took place, and when Operator 5 stepped back, Tim stared, and Diane gasped at her own image.

"I don't look like myself at all, Jimmy!"

"You look exactly like Yellow Agent 77," Operator 5 said tightly. "Now, change your clothes, Di. Here—" he brought a trim street suit from a closet—"is what you need. Tim and I'll wait outside."

Stepping from the room with the Irish lad, he trod alongside the basin where the power-boat was rocking in the river waves. They waited tensely. Nervous minutes passed until the door of the little room opened, and the girl stepped out. She came forward hurriedly, and again Tim Donovan stared his amazement.

"Perfect, Di!" Operator 5 applauded. "Here's your purse, and the credentials. The greatest danger will be your lack of knowledge of the Yellowese language. You must pretend to know nothing of it because you are American born and educated. One thing more—the biggest uncertainty. You must, if possible, communicate with me here, but—we can plan no way of your doing it."

"Wireless, Jimmy?"

"The air is still 'jammed'. It may be the only possible way, during an interval of quiet. I'll have to leave that to you, Di, but either Tim or I'll be waiting at our receiver every chance. You've got to hurry. It's almost midnight. Get into a taxi now and—"

A SHRILL ring broke Operator 5's quiet words. He strode at

once into the little room and picked up the telephone, said "Yes?" cautiously, and a sharp gleam came into his eyes as a hushed voice traveled over the secret wire.

"Jimmy! Son!"

"Dad! Dad, where are you?"

"In Washington, Jimmy! I came down with Z-7 by plane. I've slipped out of headquarters for a moment to call you. Thank God you gave me this number just before Z-7 appeared at home! You said you wanted inside information on Intelligence activities, Jimmy—and I went with Z-7 to get the chance to give it to you!"

"Lord, Dad!" Operator 5 exclaimed. "I thought you'd turned against me! Look out for Z-7—he's probably having you watched. You have—?"

"Amazing information, my boy!" ex-Operator Q-6 whispered over the wire. "The Yellow Fleet will be passing through the Panamá Canal very soon now. The entire Zone is under the control of the Yellowese. A few of our officers managed to escape and hide in Station M. You know of it, my boy—its location?"

"I know that Station M exists—for use in the most serious emergency—but I don't know its location."

"Make a note of this then, Jimmy!" John Christopher urged. Operator 5 snatched up a pencil and wrote swiftly as the details of the exact location of Station M and its hidden cables came over the wire.

"That's closely guarded information, my boy! No one knows the location of that station except General Staff and a few officers of the Canal defense units!"

"Operator 5 asked tightly: "Do you mean that Station M will be used?"

"It will! You know the Canal is secretly mined with powerful charges of high-explosive. Wires run underground from the mines at Gatum Dam to Station M. While the Yellow Fleet is passing through the Canal, the officers hiding at Station M are going to close the contacts and block the way. It's going to be done in this crisis to keep the Yellow Squadron away from our eastern coast, which would mean a second and even worse invasion!"

"Great Scott, Dad—it will accomplish that purpose, but it will also handicap the U.S. defenses to an even worse extent!" Operator 5 protested. "It will bottle up our Atlantic and Pacific Fleets! They'll be unable to reach the eastern coast! They'll be helpless! The Yellow merchant marine in the Atlantic now will send troops inland with nothing to hamper them once the invisible power destroys our coastal defenses around New York!"

"That's true, my boy, but General Staff is determined to keep the Yellow Fleet back by destroying the Canal!"

"At all costs, the Panamá Canal must be kept open for our own ships to move eastward!" Operator 5 declared. "Great Scott, isn't Z-7 acting on my recommendations? Aren't steps being taken to protect us against the Yellow heat-power? They must be taken! Our fleet must be able to move into the Atlantic and fight when the right moment comes! We must not destroy the Canal!"

"The decision of General Staff cannot be changed now, my boy! Orders have already been flashed to Station M. The officers hiding there are waiting even at this minute to set off the mines and block the way!"

Operator 5 gripped the telephone in whitened fingers that crushed hard. "Thanks, Dad! The information you have given me is priceless. If General Staff persists in its orders, then the only possible way—" His voice faded. "Keep on the job, Q-6!"

HE STEPPED out of the little room, his eyes glinting with new determination. Diane was waiting: He seized her hands and led her to the outer door.

"On your way, Di! I'm counting on you—I know you will come through. God bless you—and good luck!"

Diane Elliot's hands tightened on Operator 5's, and her disguised eyes shone brightly. She hurried out, into the darkness of the waterfront; and Operator 5 quickly turned back, signaling to Tim Donovan to follow him.

He strode to another dark door in the corner, unlocked it. Opened, it revealed ascending steps. He ran up them with the Irish lad, into a room utterly black. The air was cold and silent.

Machinery began to grind. In amazement Tim looked up to see the sky appearing above him. The ceiling of the room was sliding aside, disclosing glittering stars. Drawn by machinery, constructed of corrugated iron sheeting, it coiled on a long drum high on one wall. The glow of the night filled the large room as it opened—and disclosed a weird craft sitting near the farther wall, the drooping vanes and shining propeller of an autogyro!

"Into the pit, Tim!"

Operator 5 climbed up as the Irish lad clambered in. He wrested at the crank, and the powerful radial motor burst into action with a muffled roar. While it warmed, Jimmy Christopher jerked on coveralls, helmet and goggles; settled to the controls. Breathlessly Tim Donovan clung to the cowling as Operator 5's hand went to the drawn brake-lever.

"Jimmy! What're you going to do?"

"Play a million to one-shot, Tim! Steady, old timer! We're traveling south—top speed!"

The roaring motor swung the autogyro on its fat tires. Its great vanes circling, the ship lifted and soared into the open. It coursed out over the East River, and higher and higher Operator 5 climbed, until beyond the glow of the city. Then he drove ahead, driving toward a hidden spot where the destiny of a nation had to be decided.

CHAPTER 11
DEATH'S EASTWARD PASSAGE

HIDDEN UNDER the darkness of the open night, a man in a ragged and stained U.S. Army uniform stood on the high point of land and peered at the black horizon through powerful binoculars.

He was Major Thomas Chase, once Commander of Albrook Field, Army air base in the Panamá Canal Zone—now driven with his men into rout before the merciless invasion of Yellow-

Operator 5's automatic spat flame. A howl of pain tore from
the lips of Captain Mason as he was driven back!

ese. Now, through the strong lenses, he peered at the streak of glistening Canal—and at dark figures creeping into it.

The black, gliding shapes were the ships of the Yellowese Navy—beginning their passage into the east.

Major Chase turned quickly and ran down the slope. He ducked among outcropping rock, parting bushes as he wormed his way into a black hollow. Beneath the rugged surface he came to a steel door set into a frame of beams. His knock on it brought an immediate answer and the withdrawal of a stout bolt. He slipped through, into flickering lantern light.

Here, beneath the crest of the hill, hidden from all eyes and unsuspected, lay Station M.

In the lantern light, between the steel walls, five officers had been moving about tensely. As the door of the underground room closed, they whipped about to face the exhausted Major Chase, to hear him say: "The flagship of the Yellow Fleet, the *Tolko,* has entered the Canal!"

They peered at a panel affixed to one steel wall. To it a giant knife-switch was affixed, its open blades gleaming in the lantern light. From it a metal conduit let, disappearing through a flange in the wall.

The officers knew that that conduit trailed far across the hills, underground, down to the most vital point in the great Canal. They knew that the hidden wires which ran through it were connected with high-explosive hidden there.

The moment was approaching when, by the desperate orders of General Staff, that switch must be thrust home....

Captain Hunter Mason, once Commander of Randolph

164

Field, Colon, Canal Zone, stepped close to the giant switch. His blood encrusted hand raised to the thick handle. His steely eyes glinted at Major Chase.

"Watch!" he commanded. "Give the signal! By God, we'll stop those Yellow devils!"

GRIMLY, MAJOR CHASE turned back to the door— ducked out through the narrow cleft, and shouldered into the open. Again he mounted to the high point, leveled his binoculars at the distant Canal. Slowly and inevitably, the enemy monsters were creeping closer to the hidden explosive.

Chase's nerves tightened as the distance diminished. His eyes gleamed as he swung away again. A second time he ran down the slope and struggled through the hidden entrance to the steel door. When it flashed open, he peered into the gleaming lantern light and exclaimed:

"Close the switch in exactly one minute! The flagship will be trapped and the others will collide and disable themselves! Exactly sixty seconds and the locks will be closed behind the *Patalki!*"

Major Chase again hurried into the open. He began a breathless run up the slope, intent upon observing the catastrophic blast that would sweep destruction into the Canal. His boots slashed through long grass; and suddenly he stopped short.

Black figures materialized before him. Two shadows faced him. They stood motionless as phantoms, the starlight glinting in their eyes. Yellowese? No—they were not in uniform! Major Chase's hand snatched at his service automatic.

Instantly the taller of the two black figures sprang forward.

The Major's weapon flashed upward—and stopped as a sharp blow struck his neck. A flattened hand drove instant paralysis into his body, freezing his gun arm. Rigid as a statue, he tottered, toppled.

Operator 5 poised at the mouth of the hidden hollow which gave entrance to Station M. His hand shot out to seize the arm of Tim Donovan. He pointed into the distance and spoke swiftly.

"That direction, Tim—straight as an arrow! Get as far as you can from this place within ten minutes! Pick a hidden spot. At intervals you'll find markers indicating the course of the conduit. Open it—break those wires. Quick!"

Operator 5 shouldered into the hollow as Tim Donovan spurted off. His hands met the steel door; he knocked. Quickly he heard the gritting of the bolt being withdrawn.

HE STEPPED forward swiftly, slapping the door wide, flashing his automatic into his hand. In the flickering lantern light he saw officers startled to motionlessness at his appearance. His shadow looming black against one wall, Captain Mason was peering at his watch and slowly, slowly, bringing the blades of the giant switch toward their clips. Operator 5's command snapped:

"Open it! Get back!"

Mason's eyes jerked up—up from seeing the sixtieth second tick past. His hand did not leave the switch handle. His taut muscles jerked with the impulse to thrust the blades home. Copper glinted in the light as the knives swung—and Operator 5's automatic spat flame.

A howl of dismay tore from the officer as he spun back. Oper-

166

ator 5 leaped forward, his hand outstretched for the handle of the switch. The gleaming blades were within an inch of being closed.

"Steady, gentlemen!"

Before its menace they stood motionless. Captain Mason leaned against the wall, his wrist shattered and dripping red.

Into the muffled quiet of the steel room Jimmy Christopher spoke ringingly.

"My sincere regrets, Captain. I could not stop you in any other way. And preserving the Canal is absolutely necessary. It must not be destroyed!"

Captain Mason peered through slitted eyes. "I know who you are! You have been described to me! You're an escaped prisoner of war—a traitor—Operator 5!"

Jimmy Christopher's lips thinned. "I am Operator 5," he admitted grimly. "Do not move, gentlemen. If you make any attempt to close this switch I will be forced to shoot you down."

Mason's voice gritted. "You're allowing the Yellow ships to pass through! You're keeping the way open for an invasion of the United States from the east! Good God, man! Have you so little loyalty to your country that you'll allow an attack on our East Coast—at the cost of thousands of lives?"

"The Canal, gentlemen," Jimmy Christopher declared, his voice ringing like steel, "must remain open!"

"By God, sir!" another of the officers snapped. "You've made yourself the most despicable traitor in the history of the nation!"

"Regardless of what you think of me, gentlemen," Operator 5 insisted, "you will keep your positions. You will not come near this switch until it is rendered useless. I do not presume to defend myself from you—but I shall keep the Canal open!"

Operator 5's hand gripped the switch handle, holding it down; his gun glittered in the lantern light. He thought, as he stood facing the white faced men, holding their cold fury in the control of his weapon, of Tim Donovan scurrying through the dark of the night.

THE TOUGH little Irish lad was even at that moment running breathlessly across the hills, following the course Operator 5 had indicated. He saw, far beyond, the swinging searchlights of the Yellow ships creeping through the great Canal. He dropped to his knees, his breath beating hot, and madly probed through the rank grass. Jerking out his electric torch he played its beam over the baked ground. Desperately he sought the markers which would indicate that the hidden conduit lay directly below.

A gasp of overjoyed relief broke from his lips as his hard fingers poked at the flat top of a wooden peg driven flush with the ground. The wires stretched below him, here beneath the surface!

He jerked his penknife from his pocket, bared its largest blade, and dug frantically. His chubby hands scooped the loosened earth away. He slashed and fingered deeper, inch by inch, his nerves burning hot with anxiety to reach the buried tube. When his driving blade struck something hard, he dug even faster. The crumbling dirt disclosed a corroded tube of metal—the conduit.

Desperately he tackled it with his knife. The alloy was soft, yet resisted his blade with maddening obstinacy. He hacked, sawed, bore down with all his weight, peeling ragged edges aside. A moan of despair blurted from his lips as the blade of his knife broke off short. Desperately he bared the smaller end and again, with hastened vigor, tackled the conduit.

Operator 5, he knew, was waiting in Station M, holding the men there at bay, until he could complete this task and report the wires broken.

Panting, he stripped the casing of the conduit away, pulled with all his strength upon the two insulated wires which snaked through it. Carefully working on one and leaving the other untouched—lest the blade of the knife, cutting through both sheaths at once, should complete the circuit and explode the mines—he stripped off the insulation and hacked at the copper. At last it parted and breathlessly he attacked the second.

With the strand halfway severed, he jerked up in anxiety. He had heard the noise of running steps in the grass. He saw figures racing along the slope, the glint of rifles. His breath stopped as he snatched at his light and extinguished it. The gleam of the torch, he knew, had attracted the attention of a reconnoitering squad of Yellowese!

The black figures darted toward him as he strained back—and as the second wire parted under the edge of his knife. Instantly he whirled and ran. With the speed, the bewildering agility of a rabbit he darted down the slope.

A sharp call sounded. The beam of a powerful torch flashed after him. A rifle spat, and a bullet whined past his head. He kept running frantically, in the direction of the secret Station M.

Like a chased animal he darted into the hollow which gave

entrance to the contact station. "Jimmy!" He wormed his way to the door. "Jimmy!" He slapped at the iron barrier with stinging hands. "Jimmy! The wires 're cut! Yellowese soldiers coming!"

OPERATOR 5 had turned from the giant switch at the first sound of his name. Now he jerked the door open. Keeping his automatic leveled, he said, gratingly, raspingly:

"Get out of here quickly, gentlemen, unless you wish to be captured by the enemy!"

He darted through the door, thrusting Tim Donovan ahead, keeping the officers covered. Once cold air gusted around him, he sprang away with the boy at his side, across the slope. They became fleeting ghosts in the gloom, and then, sheltered by the thickness of the night, they stared back to see the U.S. officers crowding into the open, the Yellowese swarming down.

Outside the hollow, Captain Mason crouched, huddling out of sight as the Yellowese troops mobbed past. Quickly, moved by a grim desperation, he turned back, shouldered into Station M, strode swiftly to the giant switch. His eyes glittered as brightly as the copper when he gripped the handle and thrust it home.

No faraway thunder resulted. No explosion trembled the earth. Twice more he drove the blades into their clips; but no spark jumped. The switch was dead. The mines of the Canal could not now be exploded—due to Operator 5 and Tim Donovan.

He heard, through the open door, the strange fluttering that once before had disturbed the air. Now it was louder—a beating drone which came from the sky. He raced out, peering upward. Against the sparkling gray of the zenith he glimpsed something dark flittering: the vanes of an autogyro, spinning as the weird craft soared aloft.

Grimly, Captain Mason ducked back into the cubicle of Station M as he heard the slashing footfalls of Yellowese soldiers nearing him. He tapped the key of the telegraph sounder, desperately, swiftly, sent his message.

A quick step sounded at the door. He jerked around to see a Yellow officer leveling an automatic at him, Yellow soldiers crowding in, their rifles glittering. High pitched, clipped commands sounded, and Captain Mason backed, white faced, from the telegraph key.

Like the West Coast, like the Panamá Canal, Station M had become the province of the Yellow invaders.

INTO THE clattering confusion of the communication room of WDC-13, a startling message clicked. A breathless dispatcher flashed it to the desk of Z-7. The harried Washington chief, dazed with fatigue, throbbing with nervous strain, peered aghast at the information.

"Relayed from Station M, sir!" the dispatcher exclaimed. "Just in! Good God, sir! It means that an invasion from the east is now inevitable!"

Stunned, shocked breathless, Z-7 reread words:

PREVENTED BARRICADING CANAL BY OPERA-
TOR 5—STATION M SURROUNDED BY YELLOW-
ESE—OPERATOR 5 ALONE RESPONSIBLE FOR
SUCCESSFUL PASSAGE OF YELLOW SHIPS
THROUGH CANAL TO EAST—MASON, CAPT.,

STATION M.

Z-7's fist crashed to the desk. "Repeat orders to all headquarters and all operators to find Operator 5! He must be taken prisoner at all costs! God! This removes the last doubt that he is a paid agent of the Yellow Empire—a despicable traitor to his country! Get those orders out! Now!

Z-7 sat motionless, peering through the open door of the communications room, watching the orders flashed upon the wires. Grimly he kept to his post, organizing the details of a merciless hunt intended to result in the apprehension of Jimmy Christopher.

When, at last, a wave of dizziness overcame him, he struggled out of his chair. He was exhausted, his mind numbed by the ordeal of the last hours. Slowly he strode from his office, to the panel of the secret elevator. His haggard face was that of a broken man. A moment later he emerged in the street, and took the wheel of his waiting car. He was scarcely aware of his own movements as he drove.

The location of his home was as deep a secret as his name from the agents in his service, and he covered the way to it carefully. He unlocked the front entrance and stepped into silence: he lived utterly alone. Wearily he pressed the switch in his library—and stopped short, in complete, gaping amazement.

A young man stood in the center of the room, leveling an automatic at him. And that young man was Operator 5.

For a full moment, the dark blue eyes of Jimmy Christopher searched the smouldering black ones of Z-7. It was the Washington chief who moved first. He took slow steps toward his desk. His hand swung slowly to the telephone sitting there. The sharp gaze and the gun of Operator 5 followed him.

"You know," Z-7 declared huskily, "that the entire Service is looking for you. You know that once you are seized, the penalty will—inevitably—be death. If I take up this telephone, if I inform WDC-13 that you are here in Washington, you will—?"

"I'll use a bullet to stop you from using that phone if necessary!"

Z-7's drawn face whitened. "My boy—for God's sake, why have you come here? Why have you done this? You've turned against your country, your Service, your chief! You were as dear as a son to me, and now—"

"I came here, Chief, because—Listen! Never for one instant have I turned against my country or my Service or you. My every act and thought has been in the line of duty. I'll not try to convince you of that here and now. But you've got to *listen* to me, Chief! If you don't—the Yellow strategy will succeed!"

"You opened the way for its success, my boy—by disabling Station M."

OPERATOR 5 took a tense step forward. From his inner pocket he drew a sheaf of closely written pages and dropped them to the chief's desk—his gun leveled on Z-7 all the while.

"The papers you found at 2700 Avenue X were forged, Chief. They're a deliberate trick of the leader of the American-Yellowese espionage ring to discredit me—to trap you into making me prisoner so that I can't fight them. You can prove that with the help of our graphologists. But I'm not here to defend myself.

Chief! My recommendations for the changes in our air force equipment—are they being made?"

"The Secretary of War ordered them, but now that he's learned of your interference at Station M he's going to countermand those orders. He fears a trap."

"He must not! We have only one hope, and the re-equipment of our fighting planes is half of it. The other half is to fight back at the Yellow forces with their own weapon—their heat-power!"

"It's only a matter of hours before the Yellow squadrons open a new attack—this time on New York—"

"Listen, Chief! There's nothing mysterious about the power they've turned on us. It's a force that's been known for years— they've only amplified its use. It's nothing more nor less than directional beams of very short radio wave-lengths. I've already proved that to my own satisfaction by research. This force has been in common use, but the Yellowese have covered their use of it with diabolical cleverness, so that we could not suspect its nature.*

---

* AUTHOR'S NOTE: Operator 5 is here referring to the use of high-frequency electrical impulses, and the use of very short radio wave-lengths, therapeutically and commercially.

Experiments concerning the effects of short radio waves on living tissues have been conducted over an extensive period in the laboratories of the General Electric Co. at Schenectady, New York. Many public demonstrations of the effects have been given. Human bodies, subjected to powerful short radio wave-lengths, generate artificial fever, and this aids the body to combat disease. The pioneer work in this field was done by D'Arsondival

"Listen! The Yellowese have taken pains to keep their secret because they realize we will be able to turn the same power against them once we learn the nature of it. We know it now!

in 1890. Using the wireless apparatus then being developed by Hertz, he obtained what he called "billions of oscillations a second" and found that these frequencies, when used to pass a current of two or three amperes through the human body, produced no muscular contraction or other sensation than that of heat. The main effect of this diathermy is the generation of heat deep in the tissues. Any organ of the body, or any limb or part of the body, or the whole body to any extent required, can be heated in this way. The heat thus generated is an expression of the mechanical or dynamic force exercised by the oscillations of the ions within the tissues.

Commercially, short radio wave-lengths, of intense power, and heat-producing, are used in many ways, notably for the elimination of residual gases in the manufacture of radio vacuum tubes. Electrical furnaces make use of eddy currents generated in the fields of high-frequency coils. These eddy currents, passing through conductors, generate high degrees of heat. All conductors when subjected to the currents of these high-frequency fields, become hot. In the manufacture of radio tubes, bits of magnesium, previously placed inside the sealed glass bulb, ignite or explode, consuming the residual gases, and depositing a mirror-like film of magnesium on the inside of the tube.

Radio waves, as is generally known, penetrate almost all substances. At this moment the body of the reader is being shot through and through by radio waves broadcast from commercial antennae. These comparatively long waves have no heating effect and are harmless. The very short wave-lengths are directional in the same sense as light, and can be shot invisibly through the ether like the beam of a searchlight.

We can turn it back on them! It is our only hope! For God's sake, Chief, begin the work of making that weapon our biggest defense!"

Still Z-7 stood unrelenting, his black eyes smouldering into the glittering blue ones of Operator 5.

Jimmy Christopher drew back. "Chief, the achievement of that new defense now lies squarely up to you!"

He crossed the room, gun still leveled, and jerked aside the drapes of a window which stood open, revealing how he had entered the house. He dropped through, his gun unwavering; and his head and shoulders were framed by the darkness outside as he peered in.

"Good-bye, Chief," he said quietly. With that he was gone.

Z-7 whirled back to the desk, snatched up the telephone, dialed a connection over the special instrument with WDC-13. His voice crackled into the ear of the dispatcher who answered.

"Flash all operators in Washington! Operator 5 is in the city! Repeat urgent orders to capture him at any cost!"

He broke the connection. Again he spun the dial. His call this time went through to a special official switchboard far across Washington. Again the voice of Z-7 snapped.

"Give me the President! Connect me with the President at once!"

CHAPTER 12
DOOM IN THE WAKE

T HE DARKNESS of the lower bay of New York blanketed a steam yacht which rode the swells, with engines idling. No beacons marked her position. Her name was covered by a draped tarpaulin. No light glimmered on her deck, except when a door opened and closed quickly. Close to the greatest dry of the nation, the mystery craft which was the headquarters of the Yellowese-American spy ring lay in wait.

The slight figure of a girl stood on the dark deck, in the shadow of a ventilator. Gloom hid her while she watched a door. Her nerves burned with anxiety as she kept her post. Her skin was yellow tinted, her eyes slanted—she was, according to the credentials she carried, Yellow Espionage Agent 77.

Diane Elliot had followed Operator 5's directions minutely. Under cover of dark, nights previous, she had waited at Pier 156 on the Hudson. Silent men had navigated the power-boat *Shark*, and carried her out into the bay. Dreading every moment as an ordeal, she had passed the scrutiny of the agents aboard the headquarters yacht. Now she was desperately waiting for a gambling opportunity to flash information back to Jimmy Christopher.

She tightened when she saw the door open and a slight man step out. He strode directly to another dark door and entered. In that second stateroom, Diane Elliot knew, was the mastermind of the espionage ring—a man she had confronted during a few moments trying test for the presentation of her credentials—a man whose face was constantly masked. The radio operator of the ship was carrying him a message now.

She darted across the dark deck, to the door of the wireless room, slipped inside, and backed to the door. Every nerve tight, she pressed phones to her ears, her hand poised on the sending key. She heard the constant deafening crackle of the "jammed" ether and breathlessly waited, hoping the air would clear for one brief interval....

Each second increased the danger. Her heart beat madly when the clatter in the ether suddenly ceased. Again the way was being cleared for the transmission of a message by the Yellow Command. And instantly Diane Elliot flexed the key.

She flashed her message—and again the blanketing sputter spread. She whirled from the instrument, slipped out the door. Footfalls sounded on deck—the wireless operator was returning to his post. She darted again into the shadow of the ventilator. A torturous wonder filled her mind as the door closed and she slipped away.

Had her message reached Operator 5?

NO LIGHTS gleamed in the bleak wharf-house on the west bank of the East River in Manhattan. Waves rocked the hidden power-boat: there was no other sound in the shed.

But in the small connecting room there was a bright gleam, a rustle of movement. Tim Donovan, breathing hotly, as he sat hunched before the receiving unit of the wireless installation, phones clamped to his ears, was scribbling rapidly. He jerked up as a click sounded in the space beyond. Darting as far as the outer entrance, which was just closing, he saw a dark figure silhouetted against it.

"Jimmy!"

Operator 5 hurried to him. The Irish lad breathlessly handed him the scrawled sheet. Jimmy Christopher's eyes grew dark as he read.

BOMBARDMENT NEW YORK BEGINS MIDNIGHT TONIGHT—LOCATION HQ YACHT—D

"It just came in, Jimmy!" Tim blurted. "Gee, I've been listening for hours, and this is the first word Di's got through!"

"Midnight tonight!" Operator 5 ground out the words as he strode into the smaller room. He paused; his eyes brightened with a calculating light. Suddenly he jerked open the door of a closet and brought brown garments from it.

"Use that phone, Tim! Try to get WDC-13 on the wire! Reach Z-7 if possible! Tell him what that message says!"

The Irish lad picked up the telephone, but hesitated. "Gee, Jimmy, WDC-13 will be able to trace the call. They'll find out about this place!"

"It's too late to think of that, Tim!" Operator 5 was rapidly bringing make-up materials from the drawers of a cabinet. "I've already been spotted. Four Intelligence men followed me when I started for this hideout a little while ago. I tried to shake them, but I didn't dare take too much time. They may be watching the place now. Tim! Get that message through to WDC-13!"

Operator 5 sat tensely before the mirror, working swiftly to stain his skin, slant his eyes, alter the whole aspect of his features.

Tim, striving to reach WDC-13, watched him effecting an amazing transformation—until a voice rang over the wire: a dispatcher in the central headquarters of the Intelligence Service in Washington.

"The Chief!" Tim Donovan demanded. "Connect me with Z-7!"

Jimmy Christopher did not pause in his swift preparations. He combed blackness into his hair. Jerking up, he began to pull into the brown uniform. Tim Donovan noted, in dismay, that it was the garb of a Yellow naval lieutenant, complete to the last ornament and detail.

Suddenly the husky tones of Z-7 came over the wire.

"Chief!" the boy sang out. "The bombardment of New York is to begin at midnight!"

"What!" was the snapped ejaculation over the wire. "Who's calling? Identify yourself!"

Jimmy Christopher quickly took the telephone from the boy's hands. "Operator 5 calling, Chief. Order the short-wave beams to be played upon the Yellow Fleet at midnight! Order planes up to spot them and throw all the electrical power available into the proper directional antennae. It's our only chance, Chief! If—"

He broke off abruptly, as a sharp knocking echoed in the wharf house. He allowed the phone to clatter down, jerked open the connecting door. The heavy rapping continued at the entrance, which jarred in its frame as a powerful shoulder drove against it

"Open up!" a hoarse voice commanded. "We know you're in there! We've got you, Operator 5!"

180

JIMMY CHRISTOPHER gestured desperately. "Bar that door, Tim!" He leaped down into the rocking power-boat, with frantic quickness twisted the engine into action.

"In with me, Tim!"

Tim Donovan turned anxiously from the door, began to run toward Operator 5—and stopped. A terrific blow at the entrance had brought him up short. A sharp splintering sound chilled him. He saw that the wooden bar of the door was about to drop from its sockets.

He sprang back. Desperately he gripped the parting bar of wood, braced against it with all his strength. Tears welled into his eyes as he stared over his shoulder.

A forceful impact thrust him backward just as he heard a roar from the power-boat. He spun away as the entrance cracked open. Whirling, he saw through tear-blurred eyes, the trim white craft thrust at the pier door, then shoot out upon the black water. He felt his arms gripped as he sobbed; saw two Intelligence men spring ahead, leveling automatics, heard the cracks, saw the flashes of the shots as bullets screamed out into the night.

He saw Jimmy Christopher's fast craft flash from sight. But almost at once a second boat appeared, whipping the water in the same direction. The boy sensed that it was a patrol craft; knew it was giving Jimmy Christopher swift chase. The roaring of the muffled exhausts of the two boats drummed in his ears as he struggled to tear free of the hands gripping him.

"Easy!" a heavy voice commanded. "You're not going to break away from us, kid! It's the Federal pen for you—and Operator 5'll be there right beside you—tonight!"

Grimly Tim Donovan stared out across the black water across which lay the avenue of his friend's escape. He was stunned, realizing at last that he was now a prisoner of war....

JIMMY CHRISTOPHER closed the throttle in his sleek craft and the boiling white wake of his course faded on the blackness of the lower bay. He had plunged far past the gleam of Manhattan, with all the power his motor could give him. His desperate speed had enabled him to outdistance the pursuing Intelligence craft, but now, as he listened, he heard the snarl of its exhaust in the distance. It had not abandoned the chase.

Straining his eyes through the foggy night, he shuttled back and forth, in a grim search. Suddenly he closed the throttle again, peered toward a looming shadow on the swells ahead. Slowly he approached it, discerning the details of a magnificent yacht. No light gleamed on its deck; a flapping sheet of canvas obscured its name. It hovered there like a phantom ship.

Daringly, he swung his boat alongside. And on the instant, gazing up, he saw heads peering down at him, saw leveled weapons glinting in the starlight.

In a high-pitched voice he called out, using the clipped syllables of Yellowese.

"A ladder, quick. I am carrying a message for the master!"

A similar voice cried down: "The password?"

"I do not know the password," Operator 5 dared answer. "I am not of the Secret Service. I bring an important message from Commander Nega of the flagship *Tolko!*"

His statement aroused a chatter on deck. An officer snapped a command. Suddenly a rope ladder heaved overside. Quickly

Operator 5 made his boat fast to it, and climbed up the rungs. As he scrambled over the rail, he snapped a Yellowese salute and came to stiff attention, with many piercing eyes upon him.

Piercing eyes—and a pair which gazed in dread. The young woman known as Yellow Agent 77 stood on the gloomy deck, gazing at the smart figure in the Yellow uniform who had boarded the yacht. Diane Elliot, disguised, peered at Operator 5, disguised; and no hint of mutual recognition passed between them.

One officer faced Jimmy Christopher squarely. "Your message? Your identity?"

"Lieutenant Ensal of the Tolko, sir. I can give my message to no one but the master—alone!"

The officer's eyes sharpened. Suddenly he about-faced, strode across the black deck, thrust into the cabin. Again the eyes of the others scanned Operator 5. He remained motionless, not daring to glance longer at Diane Elliot.

At last the door flashed open again, and the officer returned. "The master will receive your message."

Operator 5 strode after him to the entrance of the cabin, stepped through into dazzling light. During the moment necessary for his eyes to accustom themselves to the glare, he heard a heavy voice command in English:

"Station yourselves outside the door!"

As the door swung shut, Jimmy Christopher turned to face the man who had spoken. He was a huge individual. His face was masked in black. Through the slits of the mask, sharp and penetrating eyes stared at Operator 5.

"Your message, Lieutenant Ensal!"

Jimmy Christopher's lips tightened. He swung one yellow stained hand to the door and deliberately thrust the bolt into its socket. He turned back, noting a more intense gleam in the masked eyes, and his right hand poised in front of him.

"My message, sir," he declared in English, "is that your traitorism is at an end."

For an instant the masked man absolutely froze. Then his massive hand whipped toward his hip.

Operator 5's hand flashed at the same instant; in one split second he had the hilt of his rapier out of its belt sheath around his waist and with a swift, flashing movement the flexible scabbard was flying through the air while the glittering streak of steel poised steadily just short of the masked man's breast.

"Lift your hands!" he commanded. The needle sharpness of the rapier drove through the other's clothing, its cold steel pricking an urgent warning.

Again the masked man froze. Then he began to back slowly. Operator 5 followed him, the *épée* never wavering.

The masked man's eyes glittered with an utterly malevolent rage.

"I became certain of your identity, sir," Operator 5 continued softly, "when I last faced you at Number 2700, Avenue X, Washington. You have played the part of an altruistic patriot while secretly planning the destruction of your own country. You have no loyalty save to gold. You wish to see the United States flooded by Yellowese so that you may put them to work in your gigantic factories for mere pittances, so you can reap stupendous profits

184

from the sale of your merchandise all over the world. That's a truth you cannot deny, is it not—*Mister Carter Case?*"

THE GLITTER of Operator 5's eyes was no less bright than the shine of his poised rapier, as he continued.

"Your so called peace flight to General Balta was a clever move, Mr. Case. You did not speak of peace in that Yellow headquarters. You reported information to aid in the strategy of the Yellow attack that is coming tonight. You planned my death. You assured the enemy of the success of the invasion. I shan't find it hard, Mr. Carter Case, to thrust this rapier through your heart."

Case peered. "You may take my life now," he said huskily, "but you'll pay for it with your own. Death for you is as certain at this moment as—"

A booming concussion, throbbing across the sea, broke into the cold statement. A terrific shock shook the yacht. The force of it splintered the cabin wall, high against the ceiling; torn fragments flew in all directions. Afterward, there was a moment of stunning silence.

The hoarse voice of Captain Uhler roared outside. "Boat firing on us! Coast Guard cutter!"

Carter Case thundered an order. "Fight it off! Sink it!"

Operator 5 waited tense. The firing of the Coast Guard cutter on the lightless yacht could mean only that the Intelligence men had sighted his own boat drifting alongside, and were driving in now to seize him.

He heard another sound now—the swift bubbling of the Intelligence craft—and then a second thunderous report. Again the yacht jolted with the impact of the small shell. And during the instant that the shock held, Carter Case acted.

He drove forward, reaching out to seize the throat of Operator 5 in his great hands. Tight muscled, Jimmy Christopher held his position, his rapier unwavering. He heard a sharp gasp, felt a tremor pass through the steel—the razor edge scraping bone. He saw the glittering blade slide into the body of Carter Case—by Case's own move—and when he stepped back, whipping up the weapon, the blade flicked off drops of red.

A strangling cry broke from Case's thick lips. He lurched back, slid down the wall, his eyes staring wide through the slits of his mask.

The steel of Operator 5's rapier had struck death into the heart of the master of the Yellow-American espionage ring.

Hearing swift footsteps on the deck, Jimmy Christopher whipped around, swiftly clicked the switch, plunged the room into darkness. He snapped the door bolt back, transferred his blade to his left hand, and leveled his automatic.

Pandemonium had swept across the deck. Men and officers were scattering in terror as the looming shape of the Coast Guard cutter materialized in the gloom. Ahead of it, the Intelligence boat was slashing across the swells.

Jimmy Christopher sprang through the darkness to the rail. "Diane!" He swung over, poised above the surging water. Below him his own boat was twisting.

"Diane!"

THROUGH THE frantic confusion no answer came to the call. But black figures sprang toward him, turned by the sound of his voice, and guns glinted in the light of the beam now shooting from the cutter, across the yacht's deck. He fired once, swiftly, and the answer was a withering fusillade. The savagery of the attack forced him to drop.

Swiftly he swung to the rope ladder. He fired upward again, keeping the rail clear, and jumped into the boat. He swung his rapier, and the keen edge sliced through the rope. Instantly he thrust the motor into action, drew the throttle wide. At top speed the craft plunged toward the open sea, its course marked by a boiling white wake.

The beam of the searchlight turned upon him. Sidearms spat bullets at him and he ducked desperately. The cutter's small cannon boomed again and nearby the water broke into bubbling turmoil as the shell crashed.

He glanced back. Men were scrambling up from the cutter to the deck of the yacht. They clambered over the rails, their bullets clashing with those of the trapped officers. The fight ended abruptly as the cutter's crew swarmed to better positions and Intelligence men added the threat of their own guns. Carter Case's yacht had been captured.

An Intelligence agent strode with another on the deck, gripping the arms of a girl. She attempted vainly to free herself, but strong hands held her. The two men peered sharply into her face, as she spoke breathlessly.

"I tell you it's true! I'm not a Yellowese. I'm an American—Diane Elliot!"

"Elliot?" The name was repeated with a crackle. "You can't save yourself by giving that name! Our orders to get Operator

187

5 also cover you. You're under arrest!"

The dismayed girl peered with tear-filled eyes across the rail, at the vanishing wake marking the way Operator 5 had fled. The hands on her arms remained tight. Hopelessness filled her, brought by the dismayed realization that she was a prisoner of war....

Out of the black depths of the east rolled the thunderous burst of a huge gun. On the horizon flame flashed. Overhead a high, clattering whistle sounded—the noise of a projectile in flight. The blood-chilling wail continued far into the distance; then fire glared once more, as it struck, and a second crashing concussion rumbled across the water.

Fast as the monitor boat could take him, he plunged away from the men who sought his life!

Midnight! Zero hour! The first shell of the Yellow bombardment of New York had been fired!

CHAPTER 13
HOUR OF DESTINY

THE DEFENSES of New York harbor roared desperate defiance at the unseen convoy of doom. The ponderous guns in the abutments at Fort Hancock, Sandy Hook, crashed out shells that mingled their screams with the banshee shrieks of the falling Yellow projectiles.

And then—then the dread power struck. Heat played into the air, penetrating to the hearts and brains of the frenzied gun crews, spreading over the metal of the cannon. Crackling orders snapped caution as the heat rose to stifling intensity. Now the explosive trundled to the guns came in drums of oil. Now great hoses played lashing streams of water over guns and walls of magazines. Again crews labored and fired their pieces, though they gasped, in the suffocating torridity, for air. The precautions allowed only one salvo after the devastating power exerted its effect. The drums of oil bubbled and began to boil. Steam arose from the water-washed walls of the magazines. The huge cannon began to glow red and bright in spite of the hoses.

Overhead roared airplanes, driving out to sea, bearing toward the position of the thundering Yellow Squadrons. And across the sky, as across the earth, the burning power played. Pilots found themselves plunging through unbreathable heat. Their lungs felt scorched, their eyes throbbed like swelling blisters.

Nevertheless they drove on toward their targets. Their planes had been stripped of every removable piece of metal, equipped with non-metallic tanks, fuel-leads, carburetors and propellers. They carried bombs in tanks of oil. Their observers saw the oil begin to boil as the steel within the liquid became heated, but still they plunged on through the night, into a hell of slashing searchlights and crashing anti-aircraft shells thrown up by the Yellow Squadron's batteries.

Above Manhattan sounded the screams of falling shells. Already, bursting projectiles had sprayed destruction across Times Square and Columbus Circle. Already, blasting explosions had rocked the Empire State Building, plunged flaming havoc into Wall Street. Overhead, enemy planes roared, launched from the flight decks of the Yellow airplane-carriers, and from them bombs streaked downward.

Millions mobbed the streets in stark terror as walls crumbled, as countless windows burst into flying fragments. And then, among their frenzied ranks played the viscid poison of cracking bacteria bombs. Upon them spread the rolling, clouding evil of lethal gases. Into the close packed blocks of buildings, flaming thermite spewed, spreading mounting areas of fire. Last and most deadly, more horrifying than railing shell or plunging bomb or misting gas, the invisible heat-power struck.

A choking temperature blanketed the city. Automobiles in the streets began to glow and blister and fume. Great buses shone red hot and then white. Trolley rails became streaks of sizzling steel. The supporting beams of the elevated railways smoked and shone and then buckled beneath their loads. The metallic spire of

191

the Chrysler building became a sparkling beacon; the skeletons of skyscrapers softened within their stone walls.

Power plants, their great dynamos burned out by the enemy beams, became smoking ruins and the great city was plunged into darkness. Sizzling gas mains burst asunder beneath the streets and added their poisonous vapors to the spreading gases raining from the sky. Communication ceased as wires melted through. Transportation became an impossibility. Suffocation and paralysis and death struck far and wide through the great city. Maddened men and women shrieked as they fought to escape a chaos from which there was no escape. Within short hours New York lay at the point of complete and utter annihilation.

FAR BEYOND the lower bay, a power-boat, a fragile thing in the midst of the storm of war, plunged across the heaving waves. Operator 5, gripping the wheel with whitened hands, drove his craft toward the flashing fire of the Yellowese naval guns while spray blinded him and the sea crashed its turmoil around him. The glare of the guns was his objective, and toward it he made with all the power of his motor.

Overhead, planes of the U.S. defense units swarmed. Crashing shrapnel was tearing them out of the sky, flaming, wrecked in midair—but scores of others took their places. Their bombs streaked down upon the Yellow sea-warriors. The enemy ships were rocking not only from the recoils of their own great batteries but under a desperate attack from the air. Alone these U.S. birds of battle were attempting to disable the Yellow ships.

Operator 5 plunged close to the side of the Yellow flagship

Tolko. He saw, rising high above its deck, a thick mast supporting a web of shining aerial wires, protected from falling bombs by flanges of heavy armor-plate. From those wires the heat-power of the Yellow Command was playing—yet no force struck back, as yet, from shore.

Despair filled Operator 5. Had the United States been given too little time to equip itself with the same devastating weapon? Worse, had the recommendations of a "traitor" not been acted upon? He closed his throttle and a surging wave, rocked up by a bomb, crashed the boat against the steel side of the *Tolko.* He clung desperately, fending to keep close, as he jerked into play a coiled rope.

Bracing himself, Operator 5 tested the hook at the end of his line and with a straining effort hurled it upward. It rose high— and dropped into the water. He pulled it in, burning with anxiety, recoiling it. Again he heaved the heavy hook. And this time, grimly, he watched it curve over the rail above.

He drew it in carefully, and a sigh of gladness broke from his lips when it caught. Gripping the strand tightly, he pulled himself up, hand over hand, his boat swirling away as he climbed.

The lurching of the *Tolko* slammed him cruelly against its steel side. Dropping bombs flamed around him as he strove to raise himself. Flying water drenched him, the thunder of big guns dazed him, sheeting fire blinded him. Yet with all the strength in his throbbing body he climbed. Inch by inch, dangling above the surging black waters, foot by foot, crashing violently against the hull, he pulled himself up, and still up— until at last his gripping hands found and clutched the rail.

He swung over, his breath beating fast. The black figures of the crew darted about in a frenzy of action. He crossed the deck, peering around sharply. Uncertainty kept him poised until he saw phosphorescent wires dangling from the shining aerial overhead, streaking down into the superstructure.

HIS HAND gripped the knob of a steel door and he jerked through it. In the blinding light he blinked at uniformed Yellowese officers standing at their stations within the great control room. Half a score were intently studying the flickering needles of giant indicators; their glances did not waver. Others were bending over charts, snapping commands.

In the center of the room an officer stood astraddle, his hand gripping the rim of a huge wheel, spoked horizontally from a vertical shaft which rested in a ball-bearing socket. Thick insulation separated the base of the mast from the steel of the floor. Sparkling wires led upward, anchored to other huge insulators.

At a sharp command, the man at the wheel bore upon it so that it turned slowly, as if overcoming the inertia of a tremendous mass. Operator 5 watched in cold fascination. Here, men were directing the heat-beams of the enemy. Careful calculations were turning its full power upon their objective. A turn of the wheel shifted the invisible shaft to compensate for the swinging of the *Tolko*. Steadily the direction of the great revolvable antenna was being maintained to exert its destruction with annihilating steadiness on its target.

Sudden determination forced Operator 5 back through the door. He peered up at the great antenna above, noting its position. He stared out across the heaving waters, and his mind registered the location of the Yellow ships of the attacking formation. They were strung in a heaving line, their guns flaring, their lengths battered by raining U.S. bombs; yet each maintaining its position. With the sight photographed on his mind, Jimmy Christopher again stepped into the control room.

Straight toward the officer at the directing wheel he strode. His voice sounded high pitched and dipped.

"Special orders from Commander Nega! A change in plans. I will execute them."

His daring statement straightened the officer at the wheel. He thrust that officer boldly aside, fastened his hands upon the cold rim. With all his strength he strained, pulling the wheel, knowing that overhead the great directional antenna was swinging slowly.

Amazed, the officer stood back, while Operator 5 braced again, pulling the wheel to a stop when he knew it was pointed directly at the ships of the Yellow formation.

The officer snapped: "This is not in our plan!"

Operator 5's high pitched answer rang: "The order of Commander Nega!" Grimly he stood his position, his hand ready to flash to his gun, glaring at the bewildered officer.

He could not know that as his hands turned the wheel the beam of destruction had swung away from New York at a moment when complete destruction of the city had seemed an inevitability. He could not know that with the diminishing of the power upon Forts Hancock and Totten, gun crews had again leaped toward their giant pieces.

It was a scene of unspeakable terror; men with clothing afire leaped for safety!

His eyes defied those of the wheel officer for a long moment of sheer tensity.

"I will verify those orders!"

Coldly Operator 5 followed the other out the door. He peered across the deck, into the flame-broken night. Grim satisfaction lighted his face as he saw a glow already enveloping the nearest ships of the Yellow formation.

Quickly Operator 5 slipped into the control room and to the wheel. Flashing his automatic into his hand he deliberately fired bullet after bullet into the gleaming socket where the giant mast rested upon its huge ball-bearings.

THE CRACKLING reports turned every eye in the room toward him. A startled officer sped to the window. Peering out, he saw the deadly shine enveloping the Yellow formation. The officer spun back from the window, whipped out his automatic and leveled it. In Yellowese he commanded Operator 5 desperately:

"Throw off the power!"

Control technicians sprang to giant switches. Blinding arcs jumped from clip to blade as contacts were broken. The vibration of the great dynamos below began to die away.

An awed silence filled the control room as the officer advanced toward Operator 5. Venomous hate glinted in his eyes—he had already raised his gun when the door flashed open and Commander Nega strode in.

"His death! Now!"

The gun in the hand of the officer pointed straight at Jimmy Christopher's heart. Yet he stood unmoving, his eyes shining with triumph, his lips curved in a tight smile. The yellow finger tightened on the trigger....

And then in the space of one instant scorching heat was playing about them all.

A paralysis of bewilderment struck the officers in the room. They stared around. Their faces became beaded with sweat as they heard the snap of heating metal, saw wires begin to shine, the knife-switches to discolor. Quickly, steel walls began to fume and glow; the room was already an oven, bringing choking torture to every man in it.

Operator 5 felt the same agonizing fever. A glazing confusion came into his eyes; his lungs stung; his heart hammered. But he smiled. Then, peering into the terrorized face of the appalled Commander Nega, he spoke ringingly.

"The defense beams of the United States! Your own power is being used back upon you!"

Blinding fumes filled the room. The steel floor suddenly became insupportable. Men whirled in the baking heat, the leather of their boots sizzling. Like people suddenly struck mad they sprang out of doors, upon deck—and had to turn their widened, slanted eyes upon a sight which filled with the terror. The *Tolko* was shining hot from stem to stern!

Unreasoning, trapped, they leaped through the shine, hurtling themselves into a steaming sea. Utter havoc seized them all as flames roared high, as the great battleship became an inferno. AND ALL up and down the formation of Yellow ships the same devastating radiance had spread!

Officers screamed as they flung themselves over bending,

melting rails. Men with clothing aflame, with shoes afire, leaped for their lives into the misting sea. Clouding fumes served to film and yet intensify scenes of unspeakable terror.

Desperately Operator 5 shouldered along with the rest to the rail. The flesh of his body felt cooked, the matter of his brain coagulated, the tissue of his lungs seared with each struggling breath. He stumbled down to his knees as flames whipped around him, fought unconsciousness as he dragged himself up, flinging forward with all his remaining strength.

Insufferable pain still filled him as he plunged overside, deep into a sea which almost boiled. Scarcely conscious of his own movements as he swam from the shining side of the doomed battleship, he automatically continued his struggle through an eternity of torture, while the water around him grew cooler. Gradually he fought free of the terrorized men fighting to float in the swells. Stroke by stroke, more and more slowly, he drew away from the *Tolko*. When his strength was exhausted, he wrenched himself on his back and floated.

He both heard and felt the concussion, which seemed to rock the ocean to its bed. It was an explosion that was echoed by another and another. He knew that the heat-beams projected from the American antennae were driving the enemy fleet down into the eternal depths of the sea. But he knew only as if in a dream....

CHAPTER 14
AFTERMATH

THE NEWSPAPERS that flooded now upon the streets of the nation brought news of victory!

YELLOW SQUADRONS DESTROYED IN ATLANTIC!

U.S. ATLANTIC FLEET TRAPS YELLOW INVADERS! ARMY IN WEST WIPES OUT YELLOW LINE! HEAT-POWER DRIVING YELLOW TROOPS INTO PACIFIC! SHIPS DRIVEN FROM WESTERN COAST BY PACIFIC FLEET!

Along the Atlantic seaboard, the dead floated in with the tide. The living, rescued from the catastrophe which had wiped out the Yellow Fleet, were hospitalized in any available space—hotels, homes, theatres, auditoriums, garages. With the cessation of hostilities, American doctors and nurses worked without sleep to alleviate the pain of Yellowese prisoners. Hatred vanished in the work of mercy.

Into the great pier at Asbury Park, New Jersey, pressed into service temporarily as a hospital, three men strode. They walked past long lines of cots upon which the wounded rested. They paused, looked down at the white face of a young man who lay quietly, his eyes closed, his mouth drawn with suffering. Not until one of them spoke did he move.

"There he is, Chief."

Z-7's black eyes glowed as the eyes of the young man on the cot opened. When he spoke his voice was tight with pain.

"When you have recovered, my boy—you must face the tribunal on charges still standing—charges of treason."

He could say no more. With his two Intelligence agents at his side, he strode stiffly away. Without glancing back his shoulders sagging, he strode from sight.

The eyes of Operator 5 closed hard with suffering.

THIRTEEN MASKED men sat in the windowless room which was part of WDC-13. A secret tribunal of the Intelligence Service, they were gathered to decide the fate of four prisoners of war.

Before them, also masked, stood their chief—Z-7. Facing them, seated erect on a bench, side by side, sat the four who were being tried.

They wore no masks; their white faces were unshielded from the unflinching gaze of the thirteen. They felt the searching gaze of Z-7 upon them.

"You have," he asked solemnly, "no defense to make for yourselves?"

No word passed the lips of Operator 5, nor the lips of Tim Donovan nor Diane Elliot nor yet John Christopher.

A deep sigh came from Z-7 as he faced the masked thirteen.

"Members of this tribunal. You have heard the evidence presented against the defendants. You have heard charges of treason against Operator 5, and you know that the same charges hold against this boy, this girl, and Operator Q-6, for aiding him. Though they've declined to make any defense, I have presented all the facts in the case impartially. The decision of their guilt, gentlemen, the punishment to be executed upon them, is in your hands.

"I will conduct the prisoners from the room while you consider your verdict."

At Z-7's signal, the four arose. They walked with him to the only door in the room. The way was opening when one of the masked men rose quickly, and spoke in a ringing tone.

"Chief, it is not necessary to withdraw the prisoners. Our decision is made. Our verdict is ready!"

Z-7 faced the tribunal. Stiffly, Operator 5, Tim Donovan, Diane Elliot and John Christopher did likewise. The spokesman of the tribunal turned glittering eyes upon them.

"We, unanimously, find the prisoners not guilty—and recommend citations for extraordinary service to their country!" A stunned moment followed. And then, from the lips of Z-7 an exclamation broke. "Thank God!"

Instantly the room was a bedlam. The thirteen crowded forward, tearing off their masks, grinning, gripping the hands of those who had been prisoners of war. Tim Donovan screeched his delight. Diane Elliot flung her arms around Operator 5 and sobbed. Z-7 gripped the hand of John Christopher and the warmth of his smile erased the sternness of his eyes. For long minutes, in that room, there was a jubilant turmoil.

Z-7's hearty laugh stilled the clamor. "If I can interrupt the celebration, gentlemen, there are two men outside who wish to see Operator 5. This is a moment I've been waiting for. Come with me, my boy!"

Jimmy Christopher, his face still thinned, his movements still slow, walked through the door. He paused in the chief's office, facing the Secretary of War and Major-General Falk, Chief of Staff. Their faces were white; and the smile did not entirely fade from Jimmy Christopher's lips as they hesitated in confusion.

"If we may have the honor, young man," General Falk blurted, "we wish to escort you to the White House. The President is waiting to tender you his sincere gratitude. He realizes—he knows—the defeat of the Yellow invasion was due—that you, more than any other single man—" The Chief of Staff broke off as anger at his own confusion seized him.

"By God, I want to shake hands with you! If you can forgive a crusty-brained old fool like me—By God, young man, you not only had to fight the Yellow Empire, you had to fight your own General Staff! Let me shake your hand!"

The Secretary of War repeated the fervent gesture. Jimmy Christopher's smile grew happier, and a sigh of pure contentment broke from his lips.

"Thank God you kept the Canal open!" General Falk roared. "We'd never have routed the Yellow merchant marine in the Atlantic if you hadn't! Our Army in the west would have been wiped out completely if you hadn't influenced them to mutiny! By God! Mutiny—treason—insubordination—military crimes, every one, and the highest acts of patriotism I've ever witnessed. Your name should be spread from coast to coast as the most extraordinary patriot and hero these United States have ever known!"

"I'm overwhelmingly grateful, General." Operator 5 spoke

quietly. "But of course everything I've done must be kept strictly secret. It's a regulation of the Service, you know—and after words like yours I'll certainly insist upon the written rule being followed to the letter!"

IN HIS sumptuous penthouse apartment, Carleton Victor, as was his custom, was dining alone. He sat at a table spread with spotless linen, gleaming with finest crystal and silver, partaking of Crowe's masterly cookery. His was the keen pleasure of an epicure, uninterrupted by even slight disturbance. That is, he was uninterrupted until the door-buzzer sounded softly.

The cool-faced Crowe answered the summons and turned from the entrance with a yellow telegram envelope in his hand.

"It's for me, sir," he said, "if you don't mind."

"I don't mind, Crowe," Carleton Victor assured him. "I don't mind at all."

Crowe disappeared in a room beyond. Carleton Victor continued with the exquisite *filet mignon* that the manservant had grilled over hickory logs. He was not aware that anyone was near until, glancing up, he saw Crowe standing before him, telegram in hand, brow furrowed with profound puzzlement.

"What in the world, Crowe," asked Victor "is the matter?"

"If I may, sir—this telegram." Crowe spoke with a bewildered gesture. "It has upset me frightfully. I've never been more worried, sir. It's from my sister in Los Angeles. It says, 'All well.'"

Victor put down his knife. "You are frightfully upset, you mean to say, because your sister has informed you that all is well?"

"Yes, sir," Crowe answered. His pointed nose twitched with

anxiety. "I can't understand it, sir. Suddenly, out of a clear sky, without any trouble at all having even been hinted, comes this message saying 'All well.' Why, sir, should my sister say that? Why should she, not alone say it, but *telegraph* it? 'All well' indeed! Why shouldn't all be well, if I may put it that way, sir? I confess, this is worrying me frightfully!"

"Crowe," Victor said sternly, "you're still persisted in your execrable habit of never reading a newspaper. That's the whole trouble. I have a suggestion. In fact, I have orders. You are to take the next and fastest express plane to Los Angeles and discover the meaning of this yourself, at first hand."

Crowe's nose twitched with happiness. "I may have my holiday, sir?"

"You may, Crowe, you may. What's more—" Victor drew a thick envelope from his inner pocket. "Here are your airplane tickets. Here's a sizable advance in your salary. I've arranged it all; I was going to tell you after this very excellent dinner. You're leaving tonight, Crowe; and I hope you have a very pleasant journey."

"Thank you, sir!"

"And when you return," Victor gave his attention again to the delicious *filet*, "I trust you'll report to me that you've read at least one newspaper."

"Thank you very much, sir!"

"Not at all, Crowe," Victor sighed. "Not at all."

As he left the room, the manservant looked back at his master, who was again dining peacefully, delightedly. He closed the door and paused while he addressed a remark aloud to himself.

"Sometimes," he reflected solemnly, "I think Mr. Victor is a little strange."

POPULAR HERO PULPS AVAILABLE NOW:

THE SPIDER
❏ #1: The Spider Strikes — $13.95
❏ #2: The Wheel of Death — $13.95
❏ #3: Wings of the Black Death — $13.95
❏ #4: City of Flaming Shadows — $13.95
❏ #5: Empire of Doom! — $13.95
❏ #6: Citadel of Hell — $13.95
❏ #7: The Serpent of Destruction — $13.95
❏ #8: The Mad Horde — $13.95
❏ #9: Satan's Death Blast — $13.95
❏ #10: The Corpse Cargo — $13.95
❏ #11: Prince of the Red Looters — $13.95
❏ #12: Reign of the Silver Terror — $13.95
❏ #13: Builders of the Dark Empire — $13.95
❏ #14: Death's Crimson Juggernaut — $13.95
❏ #15: The Red Death Rain — $13.95
❏ #16: The City Destroyer — $13.95
❏ #17: The Pain Emperor — $13.95
❏ #18: The Flame Master — $13.95
❏ #19: Slaves of the Crime Master — $13.95
❏ #20: Reign of the Death Fiddler — $13.95
❏ #21: Hordes of the Red Butcher — $13.95
❏ #22: Dragon Lord of the Underworld — $13.95
❏ #23: Master of the Death-Madness — $13.95
❏ #24: King of the Red Killers — $13.95
❏ #25: Overlord of the Damned — $13.95
❏ #26: Death Reign of the Vampire King — $13.95
❏ #27: Emperor of the Yellow Death — $13.95
❏ *NEW:* #28: The Mayor of Hell — $13.95

THE MYSTERIOUS WU FANG
❏ #1: The Case of the Six Coffins — $12.95
❏ #2: The Case of the Scarlet Feather — $12.95
❏ #3: The Case of the Yellow Mask — $12.95
❏ #4: The Case of the Suicide Tomb — $12.95
❏ #5: The Case of the Green Death — $12.95
❏ #6: The Case of the Black Lotus — $12.95
❏ #7: The Case of the Hidden Scourge — $12.95

G-8 AND HIS BATTLE ACES
❏ #1: The Bat Staffel — $13.95

CAPTAIN SATAN
❏ #1: The Mask of the Damned — $13.95
❏ #2: Parole for the Dead — $13.95
❏ #3: The Dead Man Express — $13.95
❏ #4: A Ghost Rides the Dawn — $13.95
❏ #5: The Ambassador From Hell — $13.95

THE SECRET 6
❏ 1: The Red Shadow — $13.95

CAPTAIN ZERO
❏ #1: City of Deadly Sleep — $13.95
❏ #2: The Mark of Zero! — $13.95
❏ #3: The Golden Murder Syndicate — $13.95

OPERATOR 5
❏ #1: The Masked Invasion — $13.95
❏ #2: The Invisible Empire — $13.95
❏ #3: The Yellow Scourge — $13.95
❏ #4: The Melting Death — $13.95
❏ #5: Cavern of the Damned — $13.95
❏ #6: Master of Broken Men — $13.95
❏ #7: Invasion of the Dark Legions — $13.95
❏ #8: The Green Death Mists — $13.95
❏ #9: Legions of Starvation — $13.95
❏ #10: The Red Invader — $13.95
❏ #11: The League of War-Monsters — $13.95
❏ #12: The Army of the Dead — $13.95
❏ #13: March of the Flame Marauders — $13.95
❏ #14: Blood Reign of the Dictator — $13.95
❏ #15: Invasion of the Yellow Warlords — $13.95

DUSTY AYRES AND HIS BATTLE BIRDS
❏ #1: Black Lightning! — $13.95
❏ #2: Crimson Doom — $13.95
❏ #3: The Purple Tornado — $13.95
❏ #4: The Screaming Eye — $13.95
❏ #5: The Green Thunderbolt — $13.95
❏ #6: The Red Destroyer — $13.95
❏ #7: The White Death — $13.95
❏ #8: The Black Avenger — $13.95
❏ #9: The Silver Typhoon — $13.95
❏ #10: The Troposphere F-S — $13.95
❏ #11: The Blue Cyclone — $13.95
❏ #12: The Tesla Raiders — $13.95

DR. YEN SIN
❏ #1: Mystery of the Dragon's Shadow — $12.95
❏ #2: Mystery of the Golden Skull — $12.95
❏ #3: Mystery of the Singing Mummies — $12.95

MAVERICKS
❏ #1: Five Against the Law — $12.95
❏ #2: Mesquite Manhunters — $12.95
❏ #3: Bait for the Lobo Pack — $12.95
❏ #4: Doc Grimson's Outlaw Posse — $12.95
❏ #5: Charlie Parr's Gunsmoke Cure — $12.95

www.ingramcontent.com/pod-product-compliance
Lightning Source LLC
Chambersburg PA
CBHW020418180626
46812CB00003B/1036